# Thane found Adair in the garden

"I thought you had left the party altogether." His voice came from close behind her.

"I felt like getting some fresh air," she said as steadily as possible, all too aware of his fingers stroking her neck. She took a step backward. "It's getting cold," she muttered, edging past him.

"You don't feel cold," he contradicted, taking her hand. Her breathing was shallow, her heart racing when she suddenly found her hands trapped against his broad chest. And her senses showed a traitorous tendency to respond to the hard, muscled flesh beneath the thin shirt and the clean masculine fragrance of him.

But she could not forget the pain of the past. "Stop stalking me, Thane!" she cried.

"I wouldn't have to if you'd just stop denying your own instincts."

**Kerry Allyne** developed wanderlust after emigrating with her family from England to Australia. A long working holiday enabled her to travel the world before returning to Australia where she met her engineer husband-to-be. After marriage and the birth of two children, the family headed north to Summerland, a popular surfing resort, where they run a small cattle farm and an electrical contracting business. Kerry Allyne's travel experience adds much to the novels she spends her days writing— when, that is, she's not doing company accounts or herding cattle!

## Books by Kerry Allyne

HARLEQUIN ROMANCE
2479—MIXED FEELINGS
2515—VALLEY OF LAGOONS
2527—SPRING FEVER
2593—SOMEWHERE TO CALL HOME
2647—TIME TO FORGET
2725—MERRINGANNEE BLUFF
2737—RETURN TO WALLABY CREEK
2761—STRANGER IN TOWN
2809—THE TULLAGINDI RODEO
2869—CARPENTARIA MOON

HARLEQUIN PRESENTS
743—LEGALLY BOUND
783—TROPICAL EDEN

# *Losing Battle*

## *Kerry Allyne*

# *Harlequin Books*

TORONTO • NEW YORK • LONDON
AMSTERDAM • PARIS • SYDNEY • HAMBURG
STOCKHOLM • ATHENS • TOKYO • MILAN

Original hardcover edition published in 1987
by Mills & Boon Limited

ISBN 0-373-02929-2

Harlequin Romance first edition September 1988

# CHAPTER ONE

'HAVE they all arrived yet? Is everyone here?' young Dimity Newman enquired excitedly, her hazel eyes shining and her light brown hair awry, as she burst into the compact reception area of the Wayfarer Motel on her return from school.

Seated behind the counter, her aunt Adair gave a wry half-smile for her twelve-year-old niece's eagerness and shook her head. 'Not all. Some have checked in, of course, as you can see,' she advised, nodding past the smoked glass wall of the office to the many vehicles to be seen already parked outside their individual units. 'But there are still more to come.'

'Oh, great!' Dimity greeted her answer with even more enthusiasm. 'Now I'll be able to see at least some of the horses arrive. I've been worrying all day that I might miss out.' She pulled a disgruntled face. 'I don't see why I *had* to go to school today, anyway. It *was* the last day of term, after all!'

'Maybe, although your holidays still don't officially start until Monday, just the same,' Adair felt obliged to point out.

Dimity heaved a deep sigh. 'I s'pose!' she allowed grudgingly. 'Still, if there's more to arrive...' Her expression lightened immediately and she started for the door at the rear of the room that led into their family's private quarters. 'I think I'll go across to the clubhouse to watch them unload and see what else is going on. I have to feed and exercise Gypsy, in any case.'

'Well, don't be late back,' called Adair after her, knowing how her niece was apt to forget everything else, even at the best of times, once she was with her newly acquired horse. 'You know Friday night is always one of our busiest in the dining-room.'

'I'll be back in time,' Dimity asserted so blithely before disappearing from sight that Adair couldn't suppress the rueful smile that rose to her lips. If she knew anything, it would probably be a case of someone having to collect her young niece in person to have her returning at a reasonable hour that evening!

For some time now, ever since learning that the Ashvale Polocrosse Club was to hold its annual carnival that weekend, Dimity had been in a continual state of excited anticipation. Polocrosse—a very popular Australian-devised game that was a combination of polo, lacrosse, and netball—seemed to take up every minute of her spare time these days, especially since the club's grounds were only a few hundred yards away behind the motel.

Not that her family objected to her consuming new interest. In fact, they had actively encouraged it, for of all of them, Dimity had taken hardest their move some nine months before from Brisbane to the small town of Ashvale on the coast in central Queensland.

She had missed her school friends badly, but then the polocrosse season had started again, and after having been invited to watch a match by Stephanie Britton—one of the motel's housemaids who also happened to be a player, as well as the club's honorary publicity officer—she had returned, converted to the sport, and thought of nothing else ever since. The fact that her mother, Adair's older sister Narelle, had also joined the club only added to her enjoyment. Both of them had always been keen riders even when they lived in Brisbane.

But now, with the thought of Stephanie still in her mind, Adair's lips suddenly began twitching again. At twenty-two, they were of the same age, and had become firm friends since the other girl had come to work at the motel—even if Stephanie did sometimes find Adair's total lack of interest in getting to know any of the young men of the district puzzling, not to say exasperating on occasion.

'Well, I bet you change your mind once you see some of those who'll be attending our carnival,' she had nevertheless predicted confidently, persistently, only a week ago.

'I wouldn't hold my breath waiting, if I were you,' had been Adair's lightly sardonic retort. Her experiences to date where men were concerned had left her with no desire whatsoever—a veritable aversion, in fact—to become involved with any of them again.

'Although you are going to come and watch...as well as attend the barbecue and the dinner dance?' Stephanie's voice had turned anxious.

'I—well—I know I said I would, but...'

'You promised, Adair!'

'All right, all right!' she had been forced to concede, not wanting to go back on her word, but none the less regretting the momentary weakness when she had submitted to her friend's, her sister's and her niece's persuasions to participate in the carnival's social events. 'But don't expect me to be the life and soul of the party, all the same.'

Stephanie had shaken her head in rueful exasperation. 'Don't worry, I wasn't.' Pausing, she had examined Adair consideringly, noting the wing-tipped brows above heavily lashed, deep blue eyes, the finely drawn but generous mouth, the attractively square jawline—*and* the rich chestnut-coloured shoulder-length hair that was dragged back so unflatteringly into a rough sort of ponytail that did little to enhance the elegantly sculptured bone structure beneath the flawless creamy skin. She also couldn't help noticing the drab and baggy skirt and top that gave no hint of the long limbs and shapely form they covered. 'Although you do intend to take just a little more trouble with your appearance than you usually do? Because I know you can when you want to. I've seen those photos of you in your living-room where you've got your hair loose, and you look a knockout!'

Adair had shrugged cursorily. 'That was another time, other circumstances. I'm quite happy with the way I look now.' Particularly as she went to great lengths to look as plain and unattractive as possible. That was the most effective way to keep men at a distance, she had found—not to do anything to attract them in the first place. 'However, if you feel I won't fit in, perhaps...'

'Oh, no, you're not squirming out of it that way!' Stephanie had interjected swiftly, sensing what was coming. 'You promised you'd go, and I mean to keep you to that promise! Besides, as I said, you'll probably have a change of heart once the men from out west arrive. All the girls in town look forward to them coming. They're mostly all hunks. Even if they do usually beat us hollow in the polocrosse,' she had concluded with a half-laugh, half-grimace.

'They're better riders?' Adair had asked, not because she was all that interested, but because it provided an opportunity to divert the conversation away from herself.

'Unfortunately, I have to say... yes,' Stephanie had concurred, albeit a trifle lugubriously. 'You see, although we do as much riding and have as many practice sessions as we can, it's still not the same as when you're riding just about all the time, and especially doing stock work. I mean, their horses are used to pushing cattle around—stopping suddenly, wheeling, leaping straight into a gallop, that kind of thing—so when it comes to riding-off, in particular, we're not even in the hunt most of the time!'

'Riding-off?' Adair's brows had peaked quizzically.

'Pushing another player off the line of the ball, or even out of the field of play altogether.'

'That's allowed?'

'Oh, yes! Although not to the point where it's dangerous, of course, but plain hard riding with one horse pushing against another in order to force it out of the play is certainly allowed, and is one of the most exciting aspects of the game.'

Adair had nodded impassively. 'And do you have many of these teams from the west competing?'

'Only two this year—Nannawarra and Craigmont. Sometimes Wuduru come as well, but they couldn't make it this time, so in the main it will be just teams from our local zone.' Stephanie had hunched an excusing shoulder. 'It's a long way for the others to come just for the weekend.'

'So why do they? Because they consider it an easy win?' cynically.

'No, of course not!' Stephanie had denied with some asperity. 'Originally it was the Ashvale Club that invited *them* to attend on the first occasion, and because they had a good time, and it fits into their clubs' schedules—not to mention our club being known for having well-run carnivals—they've just been coming back ever since. Besides, they don't always win *all* the events. We do have some pretty good teams in our zone too, you know. Although even if we didn't, competing against the outback teams would still be a benefit, because it's only by playing someone better than you are that you get to improve yourself.'

'OK, I'm sorry!' Adair had held up her hands in surrender. 'So they're doing you a favour,' she had reversed her claim drily.

Her friend's brown eyes had narrowed mock-menacingly. 'And maybe they'll do you one too by making you realize just what you're missing by ignoring the whole male sex!' she had bantered in return.

'That'll be the day!'

'Mmm, the day the men from the west come to town, most probably,' Stephanie hadn't been averse to taunting with an almost gloating chuckle. 'Particularly as I see that Thane Callahan and David Howell, as well as quite a few of the others, are booked in here.'

Adair had merely shrugged dismissively, and refused to be drawn into discussing the matter further on a personal basis. 'Yes, well...' had been her off-hand comment, and she had put the matter out of her mind after thankfully being able at last to proceed to steer her friend's attention in another direction.

Now, however, as her thoughts returned to the present, she found it difficult to resume the work she had been doing before Dimity had interrupted her. It seemed an uncontrollable progression that her recalled conversation should prompt further unwanted thoughts in spite of all her attempts to suppress them. Thoughts of her ex-fiancé Rolfe and their intended marriage—and the pain and added disillusion he too had eventually brought into her life.

The beginnings of her disenchantment where men were concerned had really all started with the decidedly less than happy experience of her much older sister, Adair supposed. Kind, sweet, and totally trusting Narelle. She had believed her boyfriend of the time, with whom she had been very much in love, when he said their sleeping together would only make him love her more in return. But that had meant only until their union bore fruit, apparently, because immediately he discovered Narelle was pregnant he hadn't been able to desert her quickly enough, leaving Narelle to raise Dimity with only the support of her family.

Then after that had come her gradual recognition of her own father's behaviour. Not that she didn't love him just the same, of course, but that still couldn't stop her from acknowledging the obvious. Her personable father very definitely did have a roving eye for the opposite sex. Whether or not he had actually been unfaithful to her mother over the years, Adair honestly didn't know, but at the same time Martin Newman had certainly made it evident on occasion that his interest had been well and truly caught elsewhere.

Perhaps because of her own previous experiences with her husband, plus her reasonably strict upbringing, the whole sorry affair concerning Narelle appeared to have upset and certainly embarrassed Adair's mother more than anyone, even though she had managed to make the best of it. What had proved to be the absolute last straw was the break-up of Adair's own engagement just over a year ago.

Everyone had considered Rolfe and herself the perfect couple, Adair reflected. He, tall and unbelievably handsome with his blond hair and brilliant blue eyes, and already well on his way to success in his chosen field of finance; she, intelligent and vivacious, and with her classical facial bone structure predicting that the best of her already striking beauty was still to come. They had been constant, amazingly compatible companions for months, but with Dimity, delightful child as she was, a perpetual reminder of her sister's experience, Adair had adamantly held out for marriage, despite both Rolfe's urgings that they consummate their feelings for each other in the most fulfilling fashion, and her own increasing desire to do so.

Finally, Rolfe had proposed, and Adair had accepted ecstatically. The marriage date had been set, the many invitations dispatched, the reception at a large city hotel arranged. Then her whole world had abruptly disintegrated. Just forty-eight hours before their wedding day, and with presents beginning to pile up by the score, Rolfe had suddenly informed her that he really wasn't sure he was quite ready for such a permanent relationship just yet, after all, and suggested a *de facto* liaison instead while he made up his mind.

Utter disbelief, despair, and a burning mortification—not least for the timing of his announcement—had promptly overtaken Adair, but as the minutes had passed that fateful evening, and the more he had blusteringly attempted to justify the suggestion, other emotions had also begun to make themselves felt within her.

Overriding just about everything had been anger, and not only as a result of Rolfe's action, but also with herself for having allowed him to lull her into such a false sense of security. Hadn't she previously always vowed to take anything a man said, or promised, with a grain of salt? But also, there was the rather sneaking, sickening suspicion that their merely living together was what had really only interested him all along, and that his offer of marriage had simply been a cover to temporarily disguise his true intentions.

Not surprisingly, Adair had refused to give one moment's consideration to Rolfe's suggestion, vehemently requesting his immediate departure from both her home and her life instead, and declining to even speak to him whenever he tried to contact her in the weeks that followed. The whole affair had been sufficiently humiliating already— what with his behaviour, advising guests that the wedding was cancelled, returning gifts—and it was then that she had pledged to ignore all men in

future, and thus allow none of them the opportunity ever to wreak such havoc in her life again.

Once more, though, it seemed the embarrassment of the situation sat heaviest with Adair's
mother. As if it hadn't been enough to have all her
friends and acquaintances aware that she had a
husband who, to say the least, wasn't precisely loyal,
and a daughter who was an unmarried mother, the
idea of also having one who had been as good as
jilted at the altar was apparently just too much for
her, for she had promptly set about selling-up and
looking around for another motel in a different part
of the State.

Neither Adair nor Narelle had objected to the
move. When all was said and done, pitying glances,
no matter how well meant, could become extremely
trying after a while, and a change of location would
certainly put an end to all that. Martin Newman
voiced no dissent either, making Adair wonder if
it wasn't just another instance of him permitting
his wife to make the majority of the decisions concerning their business not only because she happened to be an astute businesswoman, but also as
a form of recompense for her lack of accusations
regarding his extra-marital peccadilloes.

The only one who had protested had been Dimity,
but of course even she was won over to the benefits
of country living now, and...

'They're on their way over!' Stephanie's voice
abruptly interrupted Adair's reverie, making her
start as her friend now burst into the office in much
the same eager manner as Dimity had only a short
time before.

'Who is?' Adair stared at her blankly, not quite recovered.

'Thane Callahan and his father, and David Howell, and—and everyone, naturally!' the other girl supplied in tones of exasperated long-suffering. 'I thought I'd just slip on ahead to warn you.'

'What for? They're not likely to start wrecking the place, are they?' Adair returned drily. She raised a lightly mocking brow. 'Or was it supposed to be a cue for me to roll out the red carpet?'

Stephanie eyed her mock-direfully. 'One of these days, Adair...!' She broke off as a Land Cruiser and a station wagon pulled to a halt outside the reception area. 'Oh, here they are now!' she exclaimed, and sent the girl on the other side of the counter a speaking glance. 'Now you be pleasant to them, Adair Newman, or I'll never speak to you again!'

Adair half smiled and flexed a slender shoulder. 'I'm always pleasant to guests. It's a requirement of being in the accommodation field. You should know that.'

Stephanie's lips twisted crookedly. 'What I know is that you may be pleasant to the women, all right...but as for the men, you're usually so coolly distant, I'm surprised they don't suffer an attack of frostbite!'

'No one's ever complained,' Adair pointed out.

'They probably weren't game to...for fear of receiving an even icier stare!' shot back Stephanie with a rueful laugh.

There was no time for Adair to reply, for the occupants of the vehicles had already alighted and three of them, two men and a quite lovely girl of some twenty-five years with mid-length, ash-blonde hair and vivid green eyes, were beginning to make their way into the office. The girl was the first to reach the counter.

'You have a booking for me . . . Rachel Howell?' she enquired before turning to the other girl in the room with a half-laugh that had the merest touch of mockery to it. 'You here too, Stephanie? I'm beginning to think you're following us around.'

'Oh, no!' the girl denied swiftly, but with a slight flush colouring her cheeks that had Adair studying her in surprise. 'It's just that I work here normally, even though I've taken a few days off for the duration of the carnival. I—I just thought I'd come over for a bit of a chat with Adair because we're friends, and—and I hadn't seen her today, that's all.'

A statement that caused Adair even more surprise in view of the fact that she'd had quite a long talk to Stephanie only that morning. But since she presumed her friend must have had some reason for claiming otherwise, she said nothing to contradict her, and caught the older girl's attention instead.

'Yes, you're in Unit Fifteen, Miss Howell,' she advised, placing the appropriate key on the counter. 'It's a double . . . that's correct?'

She nodded. 'Mmm, Jill—Miss Manning—and I are sharing.'

'I see,' Adair acknowledged, presuming Jill Manning to be the slightly younger girl who was talking to another three men outside. As was Stephanie now also, she noted, with a wry inward smile to see her friend engaged in animated conversation with the most attractive of the three. Perhaps Rachel Howell hadn't been so far wrong, after all. She directed her gaze back to the girl in front of her. 'Well, you'll find your unit down at the end of the right-hand side, Miss Howell. In the meantime, though, if you'd care to fill out the registration form...' She placed a printed sheet on the counter and turned her attention to the senior of the two men in the office.

Tall and solid, and surprisingly young if the man with him was his son, as Stephanie had intimated— she guessed him to be only just nearing fifty—Egan Callahan proved to have a pleasant, friendly manner, Adair discovered, and which she found herself unexpectedly responding to, if only minimally.

'You're new here, aren't you?' he sounded with a smile as she went about checking her accommodation book. 'And considerably younger than Lois Rigby too, I might add.'

Somehow sensing the younger man beside him studying her leisurely, Adair determinedly kept her gaze fixed to the man with whom she was dealing and did her utmost to quell the uncustomary flustered feeling that seemed to assail her.

'Yes—well—I've been here about nine months now. My parents bought the motel from the Rigbys last year.' She went on quickly, 'But I see you booked two rooms, Mr Callahan. Shall I put the charges for both on the one account, or...'

'No, they can pay their own way,' he inserted with a bantering grin for the younger man.

Adair's glance remained resolutely straight ahead. 'Although there do appear to be somewhat

more of you than we were expecting,' she continued, eyeing the numbers outside doubtfully.

'Oh, the other two aren't staying here. They'll
be camping over at the grounds with the rest of our
teams' supporters,' he relayed. 'My son and I
usually only book in because we stay on for a few
days after the carnival. We know a number of
people in the district, but there's not much opportunity for socialising while the matches are in
progress. And provided, that is, that you can extend
our bookings, of course.'

'Oh, no, that shouldn't persent any problems. It's
only this weekend that we're fully booked,' she advised, handing him a key and another registration
form. 'I've put you in Unit Four—just over there.'
She indicated one in the row across from the office.

He nodded and smiled, beginning to fill in the
sheet, while Adair finally turned to face the younger
man. 'And you and Mr Howell have been allocated
Unit Five next door, Mr... Callahan?' The momentary hesitation and hint of enquiry in her tone
was due to no actual introduction having been
made, and she therefore still couldn't be absolutely
positive of his identity. As she had discovered on
prior occasions, one couldn't afford to take too
much for granted in the motel business.

'Mmm, I'm a Callahan as well... Thane's the
name,' was the wryly drawled reply.

Adair merely nodded coolly. Not that Stephanie
hadn't told her as much, but she still had no interest
whatever in his first name. However, before she
could go on, Rachell Howell, who was still in the
office, intervened.

'Oh, but I thought all our rooms would be together! Lois Rigby always used to arrange them that way,' she imparted on a complaining note. 'So why can't it be the same now?'

'I'm sorry, but your booking came somewhat later than the other two,' Adair offered excusingly. 'And as it is...' she half smiled apologetically, 'I'm afraid there are no vacant units in that particular block at the moment.'

Rachel heaved an evidently disgruntled breath. 'In that case, I suppose I have no option but to put up with it, have I?' she conceded, but with a totally unaccepting grimace as she now took an obviously less than pleased exit.

'I'm sorry, we didn't realize you were all one party,' Adair apologised again, this time to Egan Callahan.

He smiled encouragingly. 'Our fault, apparently, not yours, so don't let young Rachel worry you. In any case, she'll probably have forgotten all about it in a short while. She's no doubt just a bit tired after the journey. I'll go and see if I can't soothe her ruffled feathers.'

Adair half smiled gratefully as he took his departure. Dissatisfied guests didn't make for good business. Then she glanced back at his son, one winged brow rising in a slightly challenging gesture on realising he was still scrutinising her thoroughly.

'Yes? Was there something else you wanted?' she enquired in crisply sardonic tones. She had already given him the key to his unit.

'I thought there might have been something you did,' he was quick to return drily. 'Or aren't I required to register?'

'Oh!' She felt her face warm with a self-conscious heat brought on by annoyance with herself for having forgotten. 'Oh, yes, of course. I'm sorry.' The last was added grudgingly as she handed him the relevant form and a pen.

In acknowledgement he gave an expressive tilt of his head that she found particularly exasperating, and she glared balefully at his slightly downbent head as he started to write.

She surmised that he was about thirty-one, and at least six feet tall. He was also powerfully built, the broad shoulders beneath the blue shirt he was wearing obviously as corded with muscle as the darkly tanned forearms exposed by the short sleeves. His hair was almost black, his strong-boned face as deeply bronzed as his arms. Bordered by long, thick lashes, his eyes were slate-grey, his mouth finely etched with the corners showing defi- nite signs of a quirk, while his jaw was strong and firm, and somehow suggestive of a steel-edged de- termination that rarely knew defeat.

To Adair he seemed to exude an aura of ag- gressive virility—raw and vaguely unsettling—and, furious with herself for even having allowed any- thing about him to register, let alone affect her in any way, she wrenched her gaze away to stare outside where the others were beginning to make their way to their units.

However, a movement from Thane had her looking back at him involuntarily once more, and finding him straightening as he passed the com- pleted sheet back to her. 'Adair...that's your name, isn't it?' he questioned lazily.

'That's right,' tersely. Not that she had given him the right to use it, but then she suspected remonstrating wouldn't stop him doing so either if that was how he felt inclined.

'And will you also be at the barbecue and social tonight?'

What business was it of his whether she would be or not? 'Since our own dining-room is normally very busy on a Friday night, I doubt I'll . . .'

'Oh, yes, you will!' she was abruptly interrupted as Stephanie suddenly re-entered the office. 'You know very well your mother said you could get off about nine-thirty or so tonight, and the social will be going on much later than that.'

Adair sighed defeatedly, knowing the other girl was never going to release her from her promise even if she could somehow manage to get her sister and niece to do so. 'Yes—well . . .' It appeared the only thing she had been left to say.

'In that case, I'll no doubt see you there,' put in Thane smoothly and, raising his hand in a casual salute to both girls, took his leave.

'Well, well . . . !' chortled Stephanie immediately he was out of hearing. 'Didn't I tell you things would start to happen once they arrived?'

'Except that nothing *has* happened, or is *going* to happen!' denied Adair vexedly, adamantly.

'No, of course not,' Stephanie wasn't above agreeing, facetiously. 'Thane just happened to ask if you'd be going to the barbecue because he thought you would be hungry.'

'It might just as well have been the reason, since I have no intention of—umm—furthering his acquaintance anyway!'

'But why on earth not? I mean, Thane's...'

'Simply another man cast in exactly the same mould as all the rest of them!' interposed Adair on a vehement note. Pausing, she clamped down on her emotions. It wasn't her friend's fault she thought as she did, after all. 'So just let's leave it at that, hmm? Or...' she halted again, her lips starting to curve, 'you could perhaps explain precisely what you were about by denying you'd seen me previously today. Or have I already drawn the right conclusion after watching you—misguided girl—chatting up the good-looking feller with the dark brown hair?'

'David, you mean?' hazarded Stephanie, looking a trifle sheepish. 'Oh, he's Rachel's brother—if you haven't already guessed—and a near neighbour of the Callahans, I believe. I'll introduce you to him, as well as Jill, at the social.'

An event Adair would just as soon forgo. Aloud, she chided wryly, 'You're changing the subject.'

Stephanie grinned. 'OK, you were right, I *was* chatting him up. Can you blame me? No, don't answer that! I think I've already got a fair idea what you're going to say,' she responded to her own question ruefully. 'Besides, I think I'd better be getting back to the grounds now, anyway. So I'll see you over there later...all right?' She fixed Adair with a determined gaze as she made for the door.

Adair nodded, albeit reluctantly, and wished yet again that she hadn't been so free with her promises.

## CHAPTER TWO

TRUE to her word, Gemma Newman relieved her younger daughter of her duties in the restaurant shortly before nine-thirty that evening, and somewhat less than enthusiastically Adair made her way across to the polocrosse grounds where the open-sided clubhouse was ablaze with lights, and from where the sounds of general enjoyment mingled with those of the band that had been hired for the occasion.

She hadn't bothered to change after leaving the restaurant—after all, she was already cleanly and neatly dressed, if not particularly fashionably—and nor had she seen fit to alter her detrimental hair-style in any way. As she had informed Stephanie, she wasn't interested in attracting anyone's attention, and since her efforts in that direction had been quite successful to date she saw no reason to change now. Her friend was simply going to have to be content with the fact that she was making an appearance at all. Not that she expected most of those attending to be dressed especially grandly, in any event. By all accounts, it was their skills at polocrosse they were most keen to display, not their finery.

As she drew closer, Adair was surprised at the number of people that were actually present at the social, though, for they seemed to be everywhere. The clubhouse and barbecue area were filled to overflowing as the crowd ate, drank, talked, and joined in the dancing. The camping area beyond the horse stalls and playing fields was a mass of tents and assorted vehicles.

Keeping to the edge of the throng, Adair moved around them uncomfortably as she searched for Stephanie and Narelle. Apart from a few of the people from town who happened to play the sport, she knew no one there. She didn't count, or wouldn't, any of those visitors she had met briefly at the motel as they checked in during the day. But she began to feel more and more out of place the longer her search took.

On the point of giving up and, therefore to her relief able to return to the motel, it was she who was found in the end, by her sister.

'So there you are!' Narelle greeted her on a happily relieved note before her gaze turned explicitly oblique. 'I was beginning to wonder if you didn't intend to back out of it, after all.'

Remembering how pleased she had been only a moment or two previously at the thought of taking her leave, Adair shifted a trifle guiltily. 'Well—with Mum giving both of us time off...'

'For which she's hired replacement staff for the duration of the carnival,' Narelle was quick to insert, drily. Adding with sisterly directness, 'So you can forget about using that as an excuse for the rest of the weekend.' She paused. 'Besides, it will do you good to socialise a little for a change.'

'It will?' Adair raised an ironically disbelieving brow.

'Yes, it will!' her sister insisted confidently. Then, a little less assured, 'So tell me... what do you—er—think of our new guests?'

Adair drew a swift breath. Just what was Narelle up to now? Had Stephanie been talking to her, by any chance? 'As a whole, or individually?' she parried watchfully as a result.

If anything, Narelle appeared even more self-conscious. 'Well, to be honest, I mean—Thane Callahan.' She continued hurriedly, excitedly almost, now that she had actually said the name, 'Stephanie introduced us and... well, to put it bluntly, I think he's just divine!' She sighed expressively, then caught herself up with an abashed look, as if suddenly remembering she was thirty-one years old and not an impressionable teenager any more.

Adair grimaced impatiently, despite being able to relax on her own behalf now that she knew the direction of her sister's thoughts. Unlike herself, Narelle still retained a very optimistic view with regard to men, no matter how many other painful experiences she had endured since her first—much to Adair's vexation at times. Hadn't Narelle yet learnt that immediately they discovered she was an unmarried mother, men promptly thought of her as easy?

'So does he, no doubt!' she snapped at length, her irritation getting the better of her.

Narelle frowned blankly. 'So does he... what?'

'Think he's divine!'

Her sister shook her head vigorously. 'Oh, no, Thane's not like that at all! He's very nice,' she claimed in earnest tones.

She could tell on the strength of one meeting? Adair shook her head and sighed. 'Well, whether he is or not, if I were you I should still remember that he'll only be here for a few days before disappearing back to where he comes from ... and doubtless in the same uncommitted state he was on arrival,' she warned.

Narelle's expression fell noticeably. 'Mmm, I guess it's not long to get to know someone better, is it?'

'And particularly not when, from what Stephanie tells me, there are likely to be others with precisely the same idea in mind,' Adair pressed home her advantage.

Her sister digested her words thoughtfully and then shrugged. 'Oh, well, we'll just have to wait and see, I suppose.' There was a slight pause and her face began to take on a happier aspect. 'Although I'm pretty sure he liked me, too.'

A cynical twist caught at Adair's lips. 'He probably just likes women ... period!' she gibed. 'He's the type!'

'Well, thanks for the compliment!' Narelle promptly retorted in dry tones. 'It's nice to know my sister considers the only thing I have going for me is my sex.'

'Oh, that isn't what I meant at all!' Adair denied, aghast. After all, no one knew better than she did just how much Narelle did have to recommend her. She was pretty, considerate, well read, and had an attractive personality. 'It's just that ...' she bit at her lip, eyeing her sister uncomfortably, 'well, I wouldn't like to see you get your hopes up, only to have them dashed again, that's all.'

'Neither would I!' returned Narelle with a wry half-laugh. 'But in the meantime...' she gave a wave to someone behind Adair, 'it seems my presence is urgently required elsewhere. I promised to lend a hand in the kitchen for an hour or so, and I was on my way there when I met you.' She smiled apologetically, already beginning to take her leave. 'I'd better go, but I expect I'll see you later. Oh, Stephanie's at a table in front of the clubhouse if you're looking for her,' she advised as an after-thought before finally departing.

Adair nodded, and set off slowly in the required direction, still mulling over her conversation with her sister. When she finally located her friend, however, her thoughts promptly returned to the present on seeing who else was seated at the table with Stephanie, and she remained hovering uncertainly in the shadows for some minutes.

In view of the events of the afternoon she supposed she should have expected to discover the other girl not far from where David Howell happened to be, but certainly not that, among a crowd of others, the Callahans would inevitably be there as well!

Damn Stephanie! she thought exasperatedly. She, at least, knew she hadn't the slightest desire to come into contact with Thane Callahan. Then, furious with herself for even harbouring such a notion— had she really so little faith in her own convictions?—Adair promptly lifted her head higher, and nearly jumped out of her skin when a hand suddenly descended on to the back of her neck and a large shape ranged up beside her.

'So you finally plucked up the courage to come,' drawled Thane on a drily mocking note.

Surprised, because she had thought him to be at the table along with his father, but now realising she must have confused him with someone else, Adair recovered quickly as anger flared. How dared he presume to comment upon her actions?

'Courage had nothing to do with it . . . merely the *wish* to attend!' she retorted hotly. And shaking free of his disconcerting touch, 'Nor is there any need for you to propel me along either! I can make it to the table perfectly well on my own!'

'Because you prefer to keep everyone at a distance?'

'No, not everyone. Just some!' she sniped with a tight but explicit smile.

'Why?'

'Why?' she repeated, caught unawares, and stared up into a pair of intent grey eyes that she suddenly found extremely discomposing. 'Because I—because . . . That happens to be *my* business!' she snapped as she finally managed to drag her own gaze away, and hurried forward to the table.

By the time she had been introduced to everyone, and had deliberately ignored the vacant seat beside Thane's own chair in preference for one between his father and Stephanie, Adair's composure had returned and she was able to take stock of those present with a little more equanimity.

For the most part they seemed to be either members or supporters of the Nannawarra teams, and in the main a friendly, good-natured crowd, although it was with some of those more familiar to her that her attention remained the longest.

First, there was David Howell. Of much the same age as Thane, but with such a free and casual look

about him that she felt sorry for her friend if she
hoped to hold his interest for any length of time.
Then there was softly spoken, attractive Jill
Manning, who seemed to get on well with everyone
but had no special connection with any of them
except as an apparently valuable member of one of
their teams.

And last, although by no means least, there was,
of course, Rachel Howell. Supremely confident in
her own good looks, she reminded Adair of a queen
bee as she held sway over the conversation, in-
dulged in sparkling repartee with the men, behaved
as if all those who stopped at the table to chat or
exchange greetings only did so because of her, and
generally oozed honey over every male who came
within range—especially Thane.

Quite without deliberation, and for no good
reason that she could fathom, Adair decided she
didn't like her, but wasn't aware of the scowl that
came to her face as a result until, of all people,
Rachel herself decided to comment on it.

'Oh dear, poor Adair, she doesn't look as if she's
having a very enjoyable time at all,' that girl sym-
pathised with what Adair considered exaggerated
concern. And meaning to imply, not like she was,
she supposed testily. 'Why don't you dance with
her, Thane?' The suggestion was made as if she
only had to voice it and it would be fulfilled. 'I'm
sure she'd like that.'

She sounded just like the Lady Bountiful be-
stowing a generous gift on some poor unfortunate,
smouldered Adair, and her eyes sparkled irately.
'No, as a matter of fact, I wouldn't, thank you,'
she denied in taut accents. 'It so happens I've been

on my feet all evening, and I'm rather tired, that's all.'

'But not too tired for just one dance, surely?' put in Thane with an imperceptibly sardonic nuance as he rose to his feet and began making his way around the table towards her.

Adair cast him a glance that was a mixture of annoyance and confusion. Why was he doing this? In revenge for her attitude in the office, or was he so under Rachel's spell that she merely had to click her fingers to have him obeying? Somehow she thought the last unlikely, considering the rugged individuality he seemed to epitomise, and yet...who could tell? Her own experiences had taught her that not everything was always as it appeared on the surface. Moreover, just where on earth did Narelle fit in all this?

'I'm sorry, but really, I...' she began, only to have Stephanie cut in on her as she and David also gained their feet.

'Oh, you've got to have at least one dance, Adair!' she partly coaxed, partly chided.

Adair could quite cheerfully have hit her, but as she was now the cynosure of all eyes, and Thane was already bending over to pull back her chair, it appeared she had no choice but to acquiesce—if with ill grace.

'One, then!' she all but gritted and, pushing out of her seat, paced swiftly to the covered dancing area without a sign of her supposed tiredness evident.

Once there, she despaired to realise that the band was playing much slower numbers now rather than the disco tunes they had been performing previously, and she stiffened when Thane took her in his arms to begin moving to the music, straining to keep as much distance between them as possible.

'Relax. No one's going to attack you,' he bent his head disturbingly close to murmur drily.

'I'm relieved to hear it,' Adair quipped defensively, but made no move to allow the gap between them to lessen. She was already finding his presence unexpectedly disquieting as it was.

'And you may even discover yourself enjoying it,' he continued as if she hadn't spoken.

'Except for the fact that the only prospect I find enjoyable at the moment is the thought of going to bed!' she snubbed.

'With or without company?'

Adair flushed and drew an angry breath as she took a step backwards. 'Without, of course!'

Thane suddenly caught her back to him and, because she wasn't prepared, managed to draw her close against him before she could resume her rigid demeanour. 'The best way to forget him is to supplant him, you know,' he drawled.

Swallowing hard, Adair forced herself to return his gaze steadily. 'Forget whom?'

His slow, lazy smile had her breath catching in her throat. 'The man who caused you to retreat behind those prickly defences of yours.'

'I haven't a clue what you're talking about,' she parried with a supposedly amused, but actually shaky, half-laugh. 'And neither have you, obviously!'

'No? Then why else are you hiding behind that chilly exterior, those favourless clothes, that most unlovely hairstyle, hmm?'

'Who said I was hiding behind them?' she countered nervously, unsure whether it was the conversation or the fact that she was all too aware of his hand warm against her back, of the movement of his muscular frame against hers at every step they took, that was strangely making her feel so distracted and lacking in control. 'Maybe I just happen to—to find them appropriate.'

'Mmm, as I said, appropriate for repelling members of the opposite sex,' Thane charged ironically. 'And all because you can't hack it any more, due to life having dealt you one deflating backhand.'

It had certainly been more than *one* deflating backhand! fumed Adair. Not that she intended discussing her family's affairs with him, though! 'That's just your opinion!' she flared bitterly. Then, shrugging with feigned casualness, 'But even if it was true, why should it matter to you, anyway? Because you're not satisfied unless *every* female within sight is throwing herself at you?' A gibing tone edged into her voice.

Unperturbed, Thane shook his head slowly in veto, and both startled and flustered her by abruptly grazing his fingers against the fragile line of her jaw. 'Perhaps you just intrigue me.'

Adair ran the tip of her tongue across her upper lip. 'I don't know why.' She sucked in a steadying breath. 'And—and you're simply wasting your time, which I'm sure could be spent far more profitably elsewhere, if you think—if you think . . .' She stammered to a halt, unwilling to actually put it into words.

Thane showed no such reluctance. 'If I think I might be able to overcome your resistance.'

Strangely, her stomach constricted at the thought. 'Precisely!'

'You don't think that's my decision to make?' There was something challenging in the way his thickly lashed eyes locked with hers.

'No, I don't!' She shook her head vehemently, breaking the unnerving contact. He seemed to be turning it into a battle of wills, and that was something she hadn't anticipated, and certainly didn't want. She was already finding herself reacting far too ungovernably to that overwhelming masculinity of his now for her liking! 'In fact, I wish you'd just leave me to live my life as *I* please! And now that I've had a dance, I would also like to go home! I've had a very busy day, I'm tired, and I have to get up early in the morning to do the breakfasts!' She began pulling away from him fractiously.

'We have to be up early, too.'

'*Now*, Thane!'

'OK, OK,' he finally agreed wryly, and released her.

Expelling a thankful sigh, Adair returned to the table as rapidly as possible in order to make her farewells, deliberately ignoring Stephanie's disappointed glance at her early departure, and then set off for the motel.

'I'll walk you back,' offered Thane, catching up to her before she had taken more than half a dozen steps.

In a last superhuman effort Adair gathered the remains of her fragmented composure about her and shook her head. 'There's no need,' she asserted without either looking at him or slowing her pace. 'I'm quite familiar with the way, and I'm sure nobody's likely to be lying in wait in the bushes. Besides...' now she did look up, sardonically, 'shouldn't you really be keeping Rachel company instead?' Narelle must be mad if she thought she had a chance while that green-eyed blonde was around!

'Why? You figure she'll miss me while there are so many others only too willing to make a fuss of her?'

Her eyes widened. 'That isn't the point, is it?'

Thane flexed an indifferent shoulder. 'Then what is?'

Adair shook her head dismissively. She guessed that was their problem, or even perhaps Narelle's, but certainly not hers. She had sufficient of her own to worry about—not the least of which was her present unwanted and increasingly disturbing escort. 'The point is, I neither need nor want you walking me back, Thane! So now, I'd be grateful if you would please go back to the others and just *leave me alone*!' Her voice began to rise.

'Because you're too frightened to become involved with any man again?' he scorned.

'No, not frightened...simply totally and unalterably uninterested!' she was nettled into retorting fiercely.

'So I was right, eh?' A provoking look of satisfaction etched its way across his features, and she couldn't control the fiery flush that surged into her creamy cheeks. 'It was a man who caused all your trouble.'

Exasperated with herself for having permitted
him to goad her into revealing as much as she had—
she must be more tired than she thought—Adair
rounded on him stormily. 'No, it's the man with
me now who's doing that!'

'All because I can see through your protective
little charade?' He quirked a graphic brow.

Since he evidently meant to accompany her all
the way, Adair increased her pace agitatedly. 'That's
just another of *your* opinions! Another of your *er-
roneous* opinions!' she scoffed.

'Is it?' A slightly caustic note entered Thane's
voice. 'Then why don't we see whether it makes
any difference if we get rid of *this*!' And before she
could guess what he intended, he had snapped the
rubber band that kept her hair tied back so tightly
and tossed it away in disgust as her hair now
tumbled to her shoulders in waves of chestnut silk,
framing her face softly, and shimmering in the
silvery moonlight.

'Oh!' Adair came to a halt with a gasp of dismay
and resentment as she promptly attempted to catch
the long strands back with her hand. 'Just who do
you think you are, making changes to how I choose
to wear my hair?' Her blue eyes flashed wrathfully.
'Heavens above, I only met you for the first time
a few hours ago!'

'And it was obvious, even then, that someone
sure needed to make you come to your senses!'
Thane retaliated, undeterred, and caught hold of
her wrist to ensure that her hair remained as it was.
'Leave it alone, for God's sake! It's damn beautiful, and it's going to stay that way!'

'That's not your decision to make!' Adair could have stamped her foot in vexation at his high-handed attitude. 'The same as it's no business of yours either how I live my life! You've no right to interfere in it!' She turned on her heel and, at the fastest step she could manage without actually breaking into a run, resumed following the well-worn path through the long grass of the paddock that separated the polocrosse grounds from the motel.

With his longer legs, it was no effort for Thane to catch up to her. 'So what did he do, this bloke who apparently turned you sour on the whole male species?' he took her unawares by unexpectedly asking.

She had presumed that anything further would simply have been a continuation of what had gone before. But as it was, she merely pressed her lips together and cast him a hopefully squashing glance, and refused to comment. He hadn't honestly anticipated her doing otherwise, had he?

'OK.' Thane accepted her silence with an oblique twist to his lips and a negligent hunching of a broad shoulder. 'Then will you be coming over to the grounds tomorrow to watch the matches?'

This time it was Adair's turn to shrug, dismissively. 'With the motel full, I doubt I'll have the time.'

'Although you did apparently promise Stephanie that you would make an effort to see at least some of them.'

She inhaled deeply. And just what other information had Stephanie also seen fit to be so free with? she wondered with some asperity. 'An effort, yes,' she owned crisply. 'That still doesn't make it a foregone conclusion, though, of course.'

'Especially when one would rather hide oneself away, hmm?'

'With someone like you around, it would appear eminently advisable!' she gibed. 'That is, if I wish to retain any of my independence at all!'

'Independence ... or timidity?'

Adair slanted him a speaking glance, her chin angling higher. 'I'm not afraid of you, Thane ... or any other man, if it comes to that,' she added hurriedly. 'I simply have no intention of allowing you to dictate what I do, that's all.'

Thane reached out to thread his fingers within the long strands of her hair, the action once again making her unwillingly conscious that she was nowhere near as impervious to his touch or his presence as she would like to be—or should have been.

'Tonight being an exception, I presume,' he drawled lazily.

His meaning was obvious, and Adair pulled her hair free of his fingers irritably. 'How right you are!' she tried to impress on him. 'In future I'll tie it back with a leather thong, and then we'll see whose wishes prevail, won't we?' She allowed herself the satisfaction of a taunting smile.

'Yes, won't we?' came the smooth concurrence that should have gratified her, but which actually only made her feel slightly uneasy.

However, when a covert look from the corner of her eye gave no clue, she dislodged her suspicions with a shake of her head and approached with relief the door that led into her family's quarters from the rear of the motel.

With her fingers on the handle, Adair turned back to, if not thank him for accompanying her, then at least acknowledge that he had. Then, before she could do so, the door was abruptly swinging inwards without any help from her and she found her mother standing in the entrance.

'Oh, it's you, Adair! I thought I heard footsteps. You're back early, though, aren't you? I wasn't expecting you home for some time,' Gemma Newman declared.

Adair hunched a diffident shoulder. 'I—er—I'm afraid I was feeling a little tired, and as I have to do the breakfasts tomorrow...' She shrugged again.

Her mother nodded. 'Well, at least I'm glad to see you're wearing your hair in a more becoming style again. It certainly suits you better that way, *and* presents a more pleasing appearance for our guests, of course.'

Adair could sense the mocking look of satisfaction on the face of the man beside her, even though she refused to give him the added satisfaction of turning to see it. Instead she just gritted her teeth and kept her gaze fixed resolutely on her mother as Gemma Newman continued.

'And this is . . . ?' she prompted, looking towards Thane.

'I'm sorry,' Adair apologised stiffly for her neglect, and proceeded to introduce them, feeling obliged to add afterwards, 'Thane offered to walk me home.'

'That was considerate of him,' said her mother, sending their visitor a polite smile. And, ever

mindful of the amenities, not to mention the
goodwill of the guests, she added, 'Perhaps you'd
care to come in for a drink, or a cup of coffee,
Thane?'

Adair held her breath. If he accepted she would
murder him!

But Thane merely shook his head and declined,
'No, not tonight, thanks, Mrs Newman. I guess I
should be getting back.'

'We'd better not keep you, then,' put in Adair
swiftly—just in case he changed his mind.
'Goodnight.'

His white teeth suddenly gleamed in such a lazily
attractive smile that her heart abruptly missed a
beat. 'G'night, angel,' he drawled provokingly. 'I'll
see you tomorrow.' He inclined his head in her
mother's direction. 'Mrs Newman.' And he began
striding away.

For a moment Adair watched him depart, unconsciously noting the impressive physique, the easy
way of walking, the assured set of his dark head,
then she gave her silky hair a defiant toss and
hurried inside.

He had said she intrigued him, she recalled some
time later while lying in bed. But why did she?
Merely because it had made him wonder, and then
correctly surmise, as to the reasons for not making
the most of her appearance...or because her disdain
for males had made him think it might be amusing
to challenge her conviction?

Moreover, just what was his relationship with
Rachel? That girl had certainly behaved pro-
prietorially towards him at the clubhouse, but at
the same time it had been her suggestion that Thane

dance with her in the first place! Adair shook her head in bewilderment. It didn't seem to make sense. And even less when she recalled Narelle saying she thought Thane might have returned *her* interest too!

Of course, neither did it make sense that Thane should have been able to affect her composure so easily either! she went on to rail at herself. It was evidently something she was going to have to exercise a greater control over during the next few days, she decided. After all, the last thing she wanted, or needed, was for him to be making efforts to include her in his apparently increasing list of conquests!

# CHAPTER THREE

THE following morning Adair was up and in the kitchen by six, checking the various breakfast orders that had been given in the day before and the times they were required, then setting about preparing the meals while her mother and Narelle laid out the trays and distributed them to the guests' individual units once the breakfasts were cooked.

Normally Gemma Newman, being the qualified chef in the family, did all the cooking for the restaurant, but in the mornings either Narelle or Adair would usually take over the responsibility of preparing the food in order to give her a break, Martin Newman and Dimity usually helping by collecting all the trays and returning them to the kitchen afterwards.

And this particular morning Adair was pleased with the speed with which all the trays were returned. No doubt, she surmised, because the majority of the guests were there for the carnival and, so Narelle had informed her, not only were the first matches due to get under way at eight-thirty, but there were mounts to be attended to beforehand as well.

Whatever the reason, however, it had made it so much easier when all the dishes and cutlery had been scrubbed and loaded in the dishwashers at an early hour because of the extra time it afforded herself, and the two other young housemaids they had temporarily employed, to generally clean and tidy each of the units once the guests had either vacated them or departed for the morning.

So, on noting the two men clad in their distinctive polocrosse uniforms leave the unit at the end of the block where she usually started cleaning first, Adair headed for it immediately with her trolley and let herself in with a master key. Stripping the sheets and pillowcases from the beds first, she collected the used towels and took them all out to the trolley, her ears suddenly picking up, and unconsciously registering the conversation as two voices emanated from the unit next door where the door was half open, and which she suddenly remembered was occupied by Rachel Howell and Jill Manning.

'I'm looking foward to the dinner dance tonight,' she heard Jill declare. 'I thought the barbecue and social most enjoyable.'

'Well, it probably would have been if we hadn't had to suffer Stephanie's pathetic and embarrassing ogling of poor David all evening,' came the reply in bored tones, which had Adair's indignation flaring on her friend's behalf. From what she had seen, Stephanie had simply been bright and pleasant, nothing else!

'Not that *he* seemed to object, though, I noted,' returned Jill drily. 'However . . . you were being just a little reckless by generously suggesting Thane should dance with Stephanie's friend, weren't you? I mean, I thought you . . .'

'You're suggesting I should consider *her* competition?' Rachel broke in scornfully. '*That* frump! My God, I couldn't believe it when she came to join us! Stephanie's doing, naturally!' she inserted with a bite. 'But what a sight! I'm sure I've never met anyone before who's quite so plain and dowdy, or who hasn't at least *one* redeeming feature to recommend her. She's got absolutely nothing!' There was a slight pause, and outside, Adair's cheeks stained brightly as she gathered up clean linen and towels—and recalled the saying that eavesdroppers never heard any good of themselves. 'And *you* think it was reckless of me to take pity on her by suggesting Thane should dance with someone like that?'

'Well, I wouldn't have said she was plain exactly. I thought her features quite attractive, even though she doesn't make the best of them,' Jill commented somewhat musingly, quickly followed by a bantering, 'But... you took pity on her?'

'W-e-ll...' Rachel lengthened the word expressively, 'I must admit I thought I could only benefit by any comparison Thane would have had to make after having been in her unprepossessing company for a while,' she disclosed.

'You don't consider his walking back here with her after their dance a sign that perhaps he...'

'Might—as inconceivable as it is—have found *something* in her favour? Lord, no! He undoubtedly did that solely in order to stir me... probably for having made him dance with her in the first place!' with a laugh.

Deciding that she had heard enough—too much, in fact—Adair turned for the empty unit just as the sound of a closing door caught her attention and, glancing round cursorily to see where it came from, she recognised Thane and his father, together with

David Howell, as they headed in her direction. They were coming to collect the two girls in the adjacent unit, she deduced, and pretended not to have noticed them as she disappeared hurriedly from view.

So Rachel was interested in Thane, after all, came the unbidden thought as she went about putting the clean sheets on the first bed. As he was also interested in her? She couldn't forestall the question that automatically seemed to follow. Compressing her lips, she attempted to put all such thoughts from her mind, but only to find neither they, nor others, were quite that easy to dispel.

She now knew the reason for Rachel having suggested that dance, of course, but had that girl really been correct in her assumption as to why Thane had accepted? Because they had both been using her for their own ends? Had everything Thane said to her—and even Narelle, maybe—been a mere cover, then? A convenient disguise because he wanted to repay Rachel—to make her less assured of him, even, perhaps? In view of the disquieting effect he had had on her, Adair felt mortified. How could she, of all people, have betrayed herself to such an extent!

Abruptly, a shadow falling across the green-toned carpet had her looking up to see Thane standing in the open doorway, and, try as she might, she just couldn't prevent the leap of her pulse. Dressed in close-fitting white moleskins that outlined his muscular legs, and long, gleaming black-top boots, his broad shoulders covered by a V-necked polo shirt in what she presumed were his club's colours of light grey with a red trim, he looked so different and yet still so undeniably virile that she swallowed convulsively.

'You can't come in here!' she challenged in a tone sharp with anger—at herself for having even noticed how vital he looked—as he took a step forward. 'It's not allowed!'

Thane's mouth curved wryly. 'I doubt Steve or Gordon will have any objections,' he asserted, continuing into the room. 'I've known them for a good many years and, as it so happens, we had a drink in here with them only yesterday afternoon when they arrived.'

'That's as may be, but they don't happen to be here now,' Adair returned in her most officious manner as she finished the bed she had been working on and moved to the other. 'And that being the case, there doesn't appear to be any reason for you to be here either.'

'Apart from the fact that this is where you happen to be.'

She kept her head bent as she pulled a sheet into place. 'Why, did you want to see me about something . . . related to the motel?' The last was added rapidly.

'You believe that's the only reason I might have for wanting to see you?' he countered.

Adair drew a steadying breath. 'It would be advisable,' she declared purposely, glancing up at last. She waved a hand towards the door. 'So now will you please leave?' Her voice rose fractionally, vexedly, seeing him leaning so negligently, so calmly, against the wardrobe.

'Uh-uh!' He shook his head, lazily uncooperative. 'Not till I'm ready.'

If she'd had the strength Adair would have derived much pleasure from throwing him out bodily. But as it was, she could only threaten. 'I'll call my father...!'

Thane laughed, his teeth shining whitely against his tanned skin, and Adair felt her stomach treacherously tie itself in knots. 'Don't be idiotic!' he admonished in a humorous drawl. He paused before continuing on a slightly more mocking note. 'At least, not twice this early in the day.'

'What do you mean...twice?' Adair couldn't stop herself querying, albeit somewhat dubiously.

'I notice you're persisting with that ridiculous hairstyle of yours.'

Now she smiled tauntingly. 'As is my right! *And* it's tied with knotted leather this time...as I said it would be!' There was no way he could undo her efforts this time.

Momentarily, his dusky-lashed grey eyes held hers consideringly, then he flexed a muscled shoulder in a non-committal gesture. 'Although you are at least wearing something a little more becoming.'

'This?' Adair looked down at her plain blue, zipped-front dress, and shrugged dismissively. 'It's only the uniform we all wear when cleaning the units.'

'It's still an improvement,' he maintained drily.

'Yes—well...' She went back to making the bed. 'If that's all you came to say...' And, flicking him an exasperated glance when he still showed no signs of moving, 'Shouldn't you be at the grounds by now?'

Thane shook his head idly. 'We're not competing in any of the first matches.'

More was the pity! grimaced Adair. Then a sudden thought intruded. 'So when are you scheduled to take to the field?' she questioned as blandly as possible. She might have promised to go and watch, but just *when* hadn't been specified.

'Me, personally, or each of the Nannawarra teams?' wryly.

She had learnt the evening before that they had two men's teams, A- and B-Grades, as well as a mixed team, and now made a calculated guess about which one he belonged to. 'The men's A-Grade team, then.'

'Nine-thirty on Field One,' Thane supplied, slanting her a provoking look. 'Why, were you thinking of coming to cheer us on?'

'There's little likelihood of that, with all these units to be finished in the meantime,' she replied, doing her best to mask the disappointment his answer had brought. It appeared she was just going to have to take the chance of running across him while there, after all. Movement outside had her gaze turning in that direction and she went on flatly, 'Meanwhile, your father and...' She paused, and simply amended it to, 'Your father's waiting for you.'

Sparing a glance towards the door, Thane nodded on seeing his parent and David, as well as Rachel and Jill now, all three of them similarly dressed to the way he was, standing talking in the courtyard. That Egan Callahan should also have been a player had come as something of a surprise to Adair, but then she supposed he certainly looked fit and capable enough to play any sport.

'So what time do you think you'll get there?' enquired Thane casually as he began pushing himself away from the wardrobe at last.

'Probably not until the middle of the afternoon,' she lied. Maybe he would miss her in the crowd if he wasn't expecting to see her until much later than she had actually made up her mind to go. That was, if he did intend to look for her, of course, she amended quickly.

'It takes that long for you to finish the rooms?' Thane eyed her intently, a dark brow peaking explicitly.

'No!' she denied huffily, feeling as if she was being criticised. 'But there's other work to be done as well!'

'Well, just try and ensure there's not too much of it, will you?' he drawled and, inclining his head in a brief salute, left to join the others.

Adair's gaze followed him involuntarily until Rachel gave him a sparkling smile as she linked her arm with his, then she spun about hurriedly to continue with her work. When next she looked up, the courtyard was deserted.

Oddly, now that Thane was gone, she abruptly found the room unexpectedly cheerless and empty. Although the latter couldn't have been said of her mind! Just why had he come? she wondered. Had he ever actually said? She didn't think he had. As far as she could recall, he had merely implied that it hadn't had anything to do with the motel.

Then what had been the reason? her brain kept trying to determine. Simply a desire to continue mocking her about the way she looked? He had certainly done that! she heaved resentfully. Just as he no doubt found it an amusing way to fill in his spare time by attempting to prove that her defences against the male sex were quite capable of being breached? Not that he was likely to prove anything of the kind, if he did but know it! Adair assured herself resolutely.

*Or* . . . had it all merely been a continuation of his efforts to repay Rachel for her part from the night before? A painful lump suddenly lodged in her chest at the thought. Not that she cared what either of them did, of course! In fact, she couldn't think of two people who probably deserved each other quite so much! Nor did it worry her if both of them considered her the dowdiest female around. Since that was precisely the image she wanted to project, why *should* it worry her? But she *did* object, and fiercely, to both herself and Narelle apparently being used for their own unprincipled purposes! And so she would tell the pair of them, if necessary, the minute either of them made the mistake of trying the same again! she vowed wrathfully.

With such thoughts still very much to the fore when Adair eventually set off for the polocrosse grounds late in the morning, it was only the fact that her niece was soon due to compete that made the prospect of her time at the carnival even remotely pleasant. Dimity had been so excited and proud at taking part in her first carnival that Adair wouldn't have disappointed her for anything by not being there to watch.

When she arrived it was to find one game just being completed on the nearest field, but another two on further fields still under way, and for a

minute or two Adair contemplated the busy scene
musingly, and not a little bemusedly. There seemed
to be spectators, horses and uniformed riders
everywhere. The latter all being clad in white moleskins or white jeans and black or brown-top boots,
the same as Thane had been, but with each club's
individual colours—green, yellow, blue, orange—
visible in the various shirts, as well as on saddle-
cloths and the bandages that protected each mount
from knee to fetlock.

Deciding the most logical place to locate her niece
would be at the horse stalls, saddling up with the
rest of the Ashvale Junior team, Adair turned in
that direction. The satisfying thought also occurred to her that it provided the perfect solution
for keeping out of the way as well. She had already
spotted a number of familiar grey and red-shirted
figures among the crowd, even though she hadn't
stopped long enough to identify any of the wearers,
and she wasn't looking to encounter any more if
she could avoid it.

Unless, of course, one of the Nannawarra men's
teams—their B-Grade, she suspected—just happened to be saddling up for their next game as well!
Adair groaned in despair as she turned the corner
and discovered exactly that to be happening only
a few yards in front of her. How could she have
been so unthinking as not to have realised the
possibility? she wondered with a disgruntled
grimace. Her worst fears being confirmed on
hearing one of the men call out to Thane, indi-
cating his presence also. But with Dimity now
having caught sight of her, and singing out exuberantly for her to join herself and her mother, she

didn't seem to have any option but to continue onwards.

Nevertheless, after having greeted her niece and sister, and having commiserated with the latter on learning that she, as a member of the Ashvale C-Grade mixed team, had lost her first game, Adair moved slightly away from the group with which they were associated—partly because of a genuine desire not to get in the way, and partly in an effort to remain as inconspicuous as possible by standing half inside the nearest of the now vacant horse stalls. But where Thane still seemed to have no difficulty in locating her, even so, a few minutes later.

'You've come prepared for war, have you?' he quizzed immediately under cover of the general talk and noise coming from the preparing players and their supporters, and surveying her drab and baggy fatigue pants and matching battle-jacket with a jaundiced, sardonic eye.

'It's possible,' Adair declared, knowing she looked her worst, and suspecting he was also aware that that was exactly why she had chosen the outfit.

For a brief moment his jaw tightened, his grey eyes taking on a metallic sheen, and she was filled with a sense of amazement that she had apparently made him angry. Then his shapely mouth assumed its normal lazy curve, although there was still the faintest hint of a bite in his voice as he proposed, 'Someone should take a slipper to you!'

'Is that so?' Adair was in no mood to allow the remark to pass unchallenged. 'Well, I'll have you know that's nothing compared to what I think should be done to you...you contemptible bastard!' she grated as pungently as her own necessary undertone would permit. 'Just don't you, or your equally despicable girlfriend, ever use me or my sister again as a means of getting back at each other, or whatever, do you hear!' In her temper she turned on her heel, preparing to leave, and quite forgetting Dimity would be expecting her to remain until it was time for her to take the field.

A forceful hand on her arm soon brought her to an abrupt halt, nevertheless, and she was spun back again swiftly. 'What in hell are you talking about?' demanded Thane, grim-faced. '*What* girlfriend of mine, for a start?'

'The cat with the green eyes, naturally!' she gibed fierily. 'You know, the one who thinks she only has to purr to have everyone running after her!'

He nodded. 'I follow the description.' Pausing, he flicked a dark brow ironically high. 'But just what makes you think she's my girlfriend?'

Implying that she wasn't? That it was simply Rachel who *wanted* to be? She hunched a slender shoulder diffidently. 'You certainly jumped to do her bidding quick enough last night!'

'*Re* dancing with you?'

Adair nodded stiffly.

'Then maybe if *you* hadn't been so quick in leaping to the wrong conclusion, you might have realised I only acceded to the suggestion because it suited me very well to do so!' Thane shook his head sharply. 'But just what on earth has any of that to do with your sister, anyhow?'

Perhaps nothing, in view of what he had just claimed, but not wanting to embarrass Narelle by disclosing too much, she stammered awkwardly, 'I—well—I thought maybe you and Rachel...'

'Could have been using her also for our own nef-
arious ends?' Thane broke in to propose in a voice
heavy with sarcasm. 'Then, *once again*, you thought
wrongly, didn't you? So in future, I might suggest
you take the trouble to check your facts before
making any more wild accusations, and particularly any supposedly concerning Rachel and
myself!'

'I still don't need her patronising or pitying me!'
Adair protested defensively.

'Yes—well...' His ebony-framed eyes were expressive as they scanned her garb once more. 'I
guess the remedy to that rests almost entirely in your
hands, doesn't it?'

She angled her chin higher. 'I'm not going to alter
the way I dress just because of her!'

Thane made an exasperated sound. 'No, you'd
much rather hide from life than face it!' He drew
an audible breath and ran a hand roughly around
the back of his neck. 'You know, there's a fine line
between independence and intransigence. Unfortunately, you don't appear capable of differen-
tiating between the two,' he charged in scathing
accents before abruptly taking his leave.

On her own once more, Adair chewed moodily
at her lip as she watched her sister deliberately
engage Thane in a brief but smiling conversation—
on both their parts—before he rejoined his own club
members. So now she was intransigent as well as a
coward, was she? And all because she refused to
do as *he* wanted! she huffed. Well, perhaps now
that he had departed, he meant to stay away in the
future too...just as she had first suggested!
Although the speculation was made with none of

the spontaneous elation she would have expected such a prospect to engender, so that she was pleased, and even a little relieved, to have her thoughts and attention diverted by the sounds of creaking leather as riders mounted, and of last-minute instructions being given.

'Give 'em heaps!' she heard someone advocate laughingly, and looking up saw the Ashvale junior team beginning to move off, the six members each duly helmeted and carrying netted racquets.

'And remember to keep those elbows out of the way!' added Narelle to her daughter.

Dimity nodded and grinned as she nudged her mount into motion. The rest of the team did likewise after having received similar forms of advice from their own families and supporters.

Meanwhile, Narelle quickly made her way over to her sister's side. 'For someone who had such scornful comments to make about Thane when I mentioned him last night, you sure seem to have changed your tune quickly enough since then, Adair,' she came straight to the point, her expression part wry, part accusing, and had the younger girl's eyes widening in surprise. 'And you knew *I* liked him!'

'While I still don't!' retorted Adair promptly.

Narelle looked less than convinced. 'Although not to the extent of declining to dance with him, *or* walking home with him last night, as I heard it. Not to mention chatting away to him just now.'

'Arguing, more like!' with a grimace. 'And none of which were my idea, or to my liking, I can assure you!'

'Oh!' Narelle's face fell, making Adair wish she had worded her reply more carefully. 'You mean he's the one showing interest, not you?'

'If you could call it that,' Adair returned drily with a shrug, trying to remedy the situation. 'He probably just can't stand the thought of any female being immune to him, although I suspect he'll tire of it before long when he realises—if he hasn't already—that despite all his efforts there's no likelihood of me ever joining the ranks of those just panting for his attention.'

'Like me, you mean?' Narelle enquired on a tightening note.

Adair swallowed. Oh, lord, what had she done now? 'No, of course not!' she denied hurriedly. 'I was thinking of Rachel, actually.'

A remark that did little to lighten her sister's expression; the more so when she conceded dejectedly, 'Yes, I rather thought last night that she sees herself as the number one contender where Thane's concerned.'

Adair couldn't let the opportunity pass. 'And if I were you, I'd leave her to it. Heavens, anyone with half an eye can see he's only interested in playing the field, not in settling down.'

'With half an eye, or just totally one-eyed with regard to *all* men?' immediately countered Narelle, eyeing her meaningfully.

'More like, clear-eyed!' Adair defended. 'Just the fact that he apparently views me as some sort of challenge at present should prove that.'

Narelle looked away momentarily, and raised a hand in acknowledgement of her daughter's anxious gestures that she follow. 'Unless, of course, your claims of uninterest aren't quite as truthful as they might be,' she caught Adair completely off guard by turning back to suddenly charge in somewhat tight accents before hurrying after Dimity.

Recovering from her surprise, but unable to decide whether she felt more exasperated or amused by the accusation—the notion was absolutely laughable, after all—Adair followed more slowly.

At almost the same time the Nannawarra men's team also began heading for their particular field, and as he passed her Egan Callahan acknowledged Adair with a tip of his head and a wide, friendly smile that she couldn't help responding to instinctively. There was a kind considerateness about him that she had to admit she found increasingly disarming.

'Good luck!' she smiled in return.

Then, bringing up the rear, Thane suddenly appeared beside her once more. 'Did my ears deceive me, or did you actually wish him luck? I mean, he may be nearing fifty, but he is still male, when all's said and done,' he mocked, irony predominant.

'But, fortunately, old enough to have passed the age of being treacherous!' Adair sniped immediately. 'So why don't you just shut up, and l-leave me alone!' An unexpected and uncontrollable quaver surfaced, much to her consternation. Hell, hadn't he caused Narelle to doubt her enough already!

An unyielding hand beneath her chin forced her face back to his again, and he expelled a long breath. 'Oh, stop being so damned intense, for God's sake...and come and watch the match,' he proposed gruffly. Releasing her chin, his fingers brushed against her jaw evocatively, and flustered her with the wave of awareness that inexplicably overwhelmed her.

'I can't,' she was thankful to be able to refuse, even if with a slight croak. 'I have to watch Dimity play.'

'You can see both games from that small mound behind the two playing fields,' Thane countered with smooth persistence. 'And don't say no, because that's where a number of Ashvale supporters are already...including your sister.'

Although just managing to discern Narelle for herself, Adair still shook her head. 'Nevertheless, since it's the first game I've ever watched I doubt I'll be able to concentrate on both of them, so I think Dimity would prefer it if...'

'If she could be certain you were also among the spectators—and the best way for that to happen would be for her to be able to see you alongside her mother,' Thane interrupted to propose.

Feeling as if all choice was being denied her, Adair tried another approach. 'I don't see why you're so interested in seeing the Ashvale juniors play, anyway. Isn't your father's match more important to you?' She did her utmost to make it sound reprehensible of him to consider it otherwise.

Thane's lips merely twitched humorously, however. 'Except that I happen to already have a fair idea of what the outcome of his game will be, whereas I haven't in Ashvale's case. And since Dimity was asking me for some hints and tips earlier this morning, I'm interested to see whether she remembers to put them into practice,' he advised.

'Oh?' Adair's arched brows rose a trifle disbelievingly. 'And just why would she ask you, in particular, for hints and tips?'

'First, because she probably realised I've had a great deal more experience in the game than she has, and second, doubtlessly because she fortunately doesn't suffer from the same fixations her aunt does,' he put forward in a goading drawl. 'So, now shall we join Narelle?'

Adair pressed her lips together vexedly, not only because of his comment regarding herself, but also because of her inability to find any other argument that might preclude her accompanying him. 'I guess so,' she therefore had no option but to accede grudgingly, sighing. And in an effort to ensure his attention was diverted from herself, she sought a less contentious subject as they walked by asking, 'So which team is your father's playing against?'

'Valleybrook.'

'And you expect to win, obviously.'

Thane shrugged, his firmly etched mouth shaping obliquely. 'We certainly hope so.'

She sent him a diffident glance from beneath the fringe of her long lashes. 'And did you win your match—or matches—this morning?' surprising herself by even wanting to know.

'Uh-huh! Both of them.' His return gaze was wry as it continued to hold hers. 'I did wonder if you ever intended to ask.'

Adair promptly retreated, mentally if not physically. 'Was there any reason why I should?' she countered stiffly.

'I could always hope you just might be interested, couldn't I?'

She swallowed. 'Why would you want me to be? Your teams certainly appear to have enough supporters here as it is.'

'That's still no reason for me not to wish for one—one particular one—more, is it?' he countered with such an engaging grin that her heart fluttered waywardly.

Adair made a helpless movement with her head and waited for her pulse to resume its normal tempo. 'You're utterly relentless, aren't you, Thane?' she accused on a sighing breath. Tilting her head, she cast him a considering gaze. 'And just a little ruthless as well, I think.'

He made no attempt to deny it, she noted, but merely thrust his hands into the pockets of his moleskins and propounded idly instead, 'Maybe it's a reflection of that part of the country where I live.' There was a slight pause. 'And that being the case...'

Before Adair even had an inkling as to what he meant to do, he moved a step behind her, she felt a brief tug on her tight ponytail, and then her hair was tumbling on to her shoulders—just as it had the night before!—and she struggled for speech in a mixture of surprise and annoyance.

Thane beat her to it. 'I've been wanting to do that ever since you arrived at the stalls,' he disclosed with evident satisfaction as he calmly handed her two pieces of cleanly cut leather thong which she accepted automatically.

'H-how...?' she could only stammer bewilderedly.

He held out his other hand to show her the now closed pocket-knife that rested therein before dropping it back into his pocket. 'Didn't you know a man on the land never goes anywhere without one of those on him?' he enquired with rankling mockery.

'Even to a polocrosse match?' Adair ground out balefully.

'Uh-huh!' he drawled aggravatingly. 'Although normally only as far as the stalls, of course.'

'Of course!' she mimicked on a hotly sarcastic note. 'Oh, I could just belt you one, Thane!' And if there hadn't been so many people around, she quite possibly would have been tempted to do just that.

'Because I won't let you downgrade yourself?' He quirked an ironic brow.

'That isn't your right to decide!' she stormed. 'And if it wasn't for the fact that Dimity...!' She heaved a smouldering breath.

'I know. You'd be on your way back to the motel right now,' Thane deduced correctly, drily. 'But she is, and...' he paused as a breeze lifted strands of her hair so that her face was haloed by soft chestnut waves and curls that glinted in the sunlight, and his expression sobered, his eyes darkening as they studied her delicate features for long, suddenly tense moments ' ... you're so damned beautiful that...' His mouth curved crookedly and he shook his head, as if to clear it. 'But now is neither the time nor the place for that, so I guess we'd better just join the others.' And clasping her hand in his, he began leading her into the crowd of spectators awaiting the coming matches on the fields nearest them.

Almost trance-like, Adair acquiesced without further protest as her heart pounded in her chest.

And all because of a few electric moments and an unsolicited opinion that she was beautiful—or at least looked better with her hair loose? she pondered weakly. But that was precisely how she *didn't* want to look!

Regardless, all her previous feelings of anger and resentment at Thane's action seemed to have dissipated to such an extent that she was unable to resurrect them. Her overwhelming emotion now, for some unknown reason, seemed to be just an incredible awareness of him—and the warmth and latent strength of the fingers capturing her own—so that it wasn't until they had joined the rest of the Ashvale and Nannawarra teams' supporters, and Thane finally freed her, that she was able to regain some control.

They moved in beside Narelle, the discernibly suspicious look her sister sent her as she noticed her altered hairstyle making Adair hurriedly vindicate in a whispered aside, 'It wasn't *my* doing!', her sister's ensuing change of expression to one of disconsolateness giving her cause to wish, yet again, that Thane Callahan had never come to town.

Among the Nannawarra followers there were also a number Adair recognised, she noted; including Jill Manning, as well as David Howell, and his sister, of course. Darkening momentarily on first seeing Adair, Rachel's eyes had then widened noticeably with perception before narrowing swiftly once again in a display of discontent that Adair was startled to discover she found distinctly satisfying.

However, the players lining up ready for the umpire to throw the ball in to start the game promptly had her attention returning to the field in front of her, and as she watched her brow furrowed slightly.

'Why are there are only three from each team on the field?' she queried of no one in particular. 'Are the others reserves?'

With a shake of the head, it was Thane who answered. 'No, the game's played in a series of four chukkas in the preliminary rounds, while the team consists of two sections of three, who then play alternate chukkas.' His lips twitched. 'If you had all twelve of them on the field at one time things could become a trifle hairy. As well, by doing it this way, the horses get something of a breather, because in polocrosse each rider is allowed one mount only for the duration of the carnival.'

Adair nodded, focusing her gaze back on the Ashvale junior players now that the game was under way, although it wasn't long before she had another question to ask—this time ruefully, 'Is Dimity part of this—section?' It was difficult for her to tell who was who under their helmets.

'Uh-huh! She's the one with the number two on her shirt.' Once again it was Thane who took it upon himself to supply the relevant information. 'That indicates she's the Centre and it's her job, in the main, to act as the pivot between the Attack player, bearing the number one, and the number three Defence player, because only the number one can score a goal, and only the number three can defend goal.'

'I see.' She hesitated. 'And what position do you play?'

By way of an answer Thane simply half turned his back to her so that the red figure one on his shirt was clearly visible.

'Oh!' She flushed and bit at her lip, feeling foolish for not having been sufficiently alert to have either noticed it previously, or looked for herself. Swiftly she concentrated on the action before her once more.

And action there certainly was, she reflected, as horses and riders galloped, slid to halts, wheeled, and charged up and down the field. The ball was thrown from one to the other, caught in the relatively small nets of the racquets, scooped from the ground, knocked out of opponents' possession, and more often than not at speeds—especially in the case of the men's competition when she happened to look that way—that had Adair holding her breath, expecting the worst. In fact, there were a couple of instances when players did tumble ignominiously to earth, and even one when two riders *and* their respective mounts crashed to the ground, although not among the juniors, she was thankful to note.

Nevertheless, it soon became apparent that although Ashvale seemed to be fighting a losing battle, the Nannawarra team was definitely gaining the upper hand, the latter owing much of their success to Egan Callahan in the defence position.

'Oh, your father did play well!' said Narelle enthusiastically to Thane at the game's conclusion. 'I only hope I can reach the same standard some day. He's obviously a very experienced player and rider.'

Thane nodded. 'Not to mention being a wily one as well,' he smiled drily.

Narelle nodded and laughed, her gaze seeking her daughter as the juniors began leaving the field. 'I also thought Dimity played quite well too, considering it was her first competition game...and thanks to your helpful comments earlier, naturally,' she added with a fetching smile.

Thane made a discounting movement with his head. 'She's a good pupil, even though her team didn't win. But in time, and with more practice...'

'Mmm, she could be challenging me for a place in our mixed team,' Narelle half laughed ruefully, but still with a touch of pride in her voice all the same.

For her part, Adair spared a look at the male riders leaving the field, noting their size, and recalling the vigour and tenacity with which they had played. 'You like playing against—*them*?' she enquired of her sister expressively.

Narelle grinned. 'Against anybody! Besides, it's not necessarily the biggest riders on the biggest horses who win. It's the combination of horse and rider, and the level of communication and co-operation between the two, that's really important.'

Adair wasn't so easily convinced, but before she could put her doubts into words another voice cut in, amusedly scornful.

'I'd have thought everyone knew that!' declared Rachel, almost elbowing Adair out of the way as she arrogantly inserted herself between Thane and the younger girl. 'At least, everyone with even the most minimal knowledge of horses!'

'Well, that lets me out,' Adair had no hesitation in quipping flippantly. 'I'm not even a fan for riding horses, let alone learning anything about them.'

'Oh, that's right, I suppose you would feel out of place here, not being from the bush like the rest of us,' said Rachel, her accompanying smile distinctly feline. 'You wouldn't know anything about country life—or country people.'

Although I do know they're rarely as insufferable as you! grimaced Adair silently. Aloud, she contended in facetious tones, 'I am learning, however!' An explicit glance was flicked in Thane's direction. 'I mean, I do know that men on the land never go anywhere without a knife of some kind, for instance.'

Thane's return gaze was blithely impenitent, but not so Rachel's comment.

'Which is hardly knowledge of the kind I was implying!' she scoffed.

Adair simply hunched an indifferent shoulder and turned to resume her conversation with her sister. Not only was she definitely not interested in anything else Rachel might have to say, but with that girl showing an obvious determination to capture Thane's attention, she was more than happy to have some distance put between herself and Thane in view of her earlier disquieting reactions.

But soon, after they had all returned to the stalls in order to congratulate or commiserate with their respective teams, everyone gradually began making their way back to the clubhouse area for lunch. Seizing the opportunity, Adair ensured she disappeared swiftly into the crowd, her eyes seeking one particular figure in the familiar aqua and black horizontally banded Ashvale colours.

Where *was* Stephanie? she all but groaned when she failed to locate the other girl, then heaved a sigh of relief when, as it happened, she almost bumped into her only a few minutes later.

'Hi! I'm glad you made it,' Stephanie greeted her warmly. 'Did you see the last match? What did you think of it?'

Not wanting to waste time by asking which of the matches she was referring to, Adair just nodded and ventured, 'It was very good.' Then, knowing it would be expected of her, 'And how about your match this morning? Did you win?' Stephanie was a member of Ashvale's B-Grade mixed team.

'Just!' the other girl laughed graphically. 'I don't like our chances for this afternoon, though. We come up against Burrai, and their mixed team seems to be getting it all together at the moment.'

'I see.' Adair looked duly sympathetic. She paused before rushing on, 'However, there was something I wanted to ask you.'

'About the game, you mean? Ask away.'

'N-no...about the—er—dinner dance this evening, as a matter of fact.'

Stephanie's brown eyes narrowed suspiciously. 'Now, Adair, you're not going to try and back out of it at this late date, are you?'

Adair swallowed. 'Not exactly. I was just wondering where, or—or with whom I'm supposed to be sitting, that's all.'

Stephanie shrugged, looking surprised. 'You'll be sitting with me, of course.'

'And where will that be?' drily.

Her friend laughed. 'Oh, now I understand. Well, since I—er—had my eye on David, I arranged for us to sit at the same table as the Howells and the Callahans, among others.'

Adair closed her eyes in despair. When she opened them again, it was to gaze anxiously at the other girl. 'Could you do me a favour and change me to another table?'

'But why? Oh, Adair, you're not...'

'Please, Stephanie!'

Stephanie shook her head helplessly. 'But I couldn't, even if I wanted to! I'm only the publicity officer for the club. The secretary has charge of all the seating for tonight, and she'll scream blue murder if anyone asks her to start making alterations now! She had enough trouble getting it all sorted out to everyone's satisfaction in the first place.'

Adair pressed her lips together and sighed. 'So there's no chance...?'

'I'm sorry,' Stephanie apologised ruefully. 'Although when I saw you with your hair loose, I must admit I thought that maybe you...'

'Except that having it this way wasn't *my* idea!' Adair interposed with a grimace.

'Oh!' Stephanie's lips twitched irrepressibly. 'Thane...?'

'How did you guess?' caustically. 'That man would have to be...'

'About to join us,' put in her friend swiftly, warningly.

'What? Oh, no!' Adair gazed skywards in dismay before turning to see for herself.

Reaching them, Thane smiled lazily down at her. Perturbingly from Adair's point of view, as she felt her pulse abruptly race. 'You wouldn't have been thinking of returning to the motel without stopping for lunch, I hope,' he murmured in what she could only call provoking tones. And just as if he could now read her damned mind!

Adair expelled a heavy breath. 'Would I dare indulge in such wishful thinking?' she quipped, albeit in rather defeated tones.

## CHAPTER FOUR

NOR was lunch all she had been pressured into staying for, Adair recalled as she reluctantly made ready for the dinner dance that evening. She had also been badgered into remaining to watch not only Stephanie's team in action, but Thane's as well, although on those occasions it had been her friend who had made it impossible for her leave.

And if she was strictly honest with herself, Adair had to admit that she hadn't totally regretted having stayed, for despite having had a sneaking suspicion prior to the game that she was secretly half hoping Thane's team, at least, might lose, by the time play was concluded she had found herself applauding as enthusiastically as everyone else. Individually excellent, as a team the Nannawarra men's A-grade had proved to be unbeatable, and thoroughly deserving of their place in the finals the next day, she'd had to concede.

Now, however, as she surveyed the contents of her wardrobe, she concentrated on the immediate. It wasn't to be a dressy affair, she knew, and her hand automatically reached for the plain beige dress she had planned to wear, then swung towards one of two-toned blue that had, in the past, been something of a favourite. So Rachel had taken pity on her, thought her dowdy, without one redeeming feature, and no competition, did she? Well, just maybe she would show Rachel Howell she wasn't always the frump that girl considered her to be, and thereby... Adair caught herself up with a gasp. And thereby have Thane believing he had brought about the change, no doubt!

With a resolute compressing of her lips she extracted the three-quarter sleeved, loosely belted tunic of beige cotton and donned it almost defiantly. What did she care what Rachel—or Thane for that matter—thought of her? They were only in Ashvale for the weekend, or a few days longer in Thane's case, and then they would be gone and everything would return to normal again—thank goodness! Wasn't it bad enough that she had been forced into deciding to leave her hair loose? Since Thane would doubtlessly ensure it ended up that way no matter how she tried to prevent it, she had supposed she might as well leave it down and save the destruction of another of her fasteners at least!

There was a tap on her door and Gemma Newman put her head into the room. 'Thane's here to collect you, Adair,' she advised casually. 'Have a nice time, won't you? Your father and I are just off to the restaurant.'

'What do you mean, he's here to collect me?' Adair burst out, frowning, before her mother could take her leave. 'I was intending to drive down to the hotel on my own.' The old and large two-storeyed Victoria Hotel was the only venue in town with sufficient room and facilities capable of catering for such a function.

Gemma Newman's demeanour became a little anxious. 'Well, since he *is* here—and it would be nicer for you not to arrive alone, I would have thought...' She shrugged.

Knowing her mother was keen to get going, Adair half smiled reassuringly. 'Yes—well—don't you worry about it, Mum. I'll sort it out.'

Obviously relieved, Gemma Newman took her departure. Her daughter, meanwhile, scowled stormily. If Thane Callahan thought he was going to take over *every* aspect of her life while he was in town, he had a shock coming! Adair fumed, and purposely took her time to finish dressing.

When she did finally enter the living-room, it was to find Thane studying some family photographs grouped on a bookcase, and since he hadn't immediately registered her arrival, Adair took stock of him silently for a moment.

He was dressed in pale grey pants, blue shirt and tie, and a darker blue jacket that set off his broad shoulders to advantage. He looked ruggedly handsome, and she felt a peculiar tightness in her stomach as her eyes travelled the muscular length of him in ungovernable appreciation. Then her gaze suddenly connected with his, and she flushed with mortification at having been caught evaluating him so openly.

'So you finally managed to make it?' he drawled immediately, and glanced significantly at the watch that encircled his wrist.

Striving to regain her shattered composure, Adair hunched a negligent shoulder. 'You didn't *have* to wait. I didn't ask for an escort, and...' she hesitated briefly, 'nor do I require one.'

'Perhaps not,' he was willing to allow. 'Although it does seem a trifle unnecessary to use two vehicles when one will suffice, and the station wagon's already waiting outside.'

'None the less, I would still prefer...'

'Oh, for God's sake, just come and get in the car, will you?' Thane intervened roughly, shaking his head in disbelief. He began pacing towards her lithely, and Adair stiffened. 'I wouldn't be surprised if Narelle and Dimity, not to mention the old man, had decided it would be quicker to walk by now!'

'They're waiting in the car?' She bit her lip in consternation, feeling even more discomfited now for having delayed so long.

'Of course!' A mocking brow swept upwards. 'Or did you think I only had seduction on my mind?'

Twin circles of colour stained Adair's cheeks once more, as she was aware that something along just those lines had been in her thoughts. 'N-no, naturally not!' she denied with a stammer, but doing her utmost to sound scornful rather than guilty.

'Then there's no reason for you not to come with us, is there?' He promptly began guiding her into the hallway with a hand at her elbow, and she was unbelievably conscious of his touch, of the clean and slightly tangy smell of his aftershave, and of his powerful form so close to hers.

'I—well, except that I prefer—to have the choice of being able to leave when *I* want to, that's all!' she managed to protest at last, pulling free of him.

Thane suddenly swung to face her, trapping her against the wall with a hand resting against it on either side of her head. 'Like... half-way through the evening?' His own head lowered and he shook it slowly. 'Uh-uh! Tonight you won't be running away, angel.'

Adair licked at her lips and valiantly held his disconcertingly close gaze. 'As with everything else, whether I stay or leave—and for whatever reason— is *my* decision to make, Thane, not yours!' She drew a shaky breath. 'And as I've said before, I'm—not afraid of you either, if that's what you're mistakenly thinking.'

'I wouldn't want it any other way,' he averred in a suddenly deeper, more resonant tone as he crooked a finger beneath her chin, tilting it higher, and his shapely mouth brushed against hers in a brief but sensuous caress before she could evade it. 'So now shall we go?' He inclined his head enquiringly, his sable-lashed eyes continuing to hold hers.

Feeling helpless to do otherwise, and not trusting herself to speak, Adair turned for the door, nodding weakly. Any further protests would merely serve to gainsay her own claim. And she wasn't afraid of him! she reiterated to herself. A bubble of faintly hysterical laughter caught in her throat. It was the effect he seemed capable of having on her that she was coming to fear!

Thane's momentary possession of her lips had been the first kiss she had received from a man since her break with Rolfe a year before, and she had been neither prepared for, nor able to control, the maelstrom of perturbing feelings it had generated within her. She hadn't expected, or ever wanted, to be so affected by any man again. And definitely not to the extent that Thane seemed able to disturb her, with such ease. Why, not even Rolfe had succeeded in making her quite so aware of him—his touch, the feel of his lips on hers, the sheer maleness of him—as Thane had in such a short time, she reflected distractedly as they made their way outside.

The massive arched and wood-panelled dining-room of the hotel that had been reserved for the occasion, as well as the paved and colourfully lit beer garden just beyond the three sets of tall french doors that gave on to it, was already filled with people when they arrived. The tables, mostly set for a dozen or so, were arranged in a semi-circle about a cleared area that had been left for dancing, which was even then being utilised by a few of the younger ones present. The music was provided by the same quartet that had played at the barbecue the night before.

Other people were either already seated at their designated tables, or else moving from one to the other, discussing the events of the day—the wins and the losses, the goals that should have been scored but weren't, the likely outcome of the finals the following day—or just conversing generally.

'Over here, Thane!' hailed a distinctive feminine voice suddenly, and on searching the crowd Adair saw Rachel beckoning gaily to them from a table that was already nearly filled. Well, beckoning to Thane at least, she amended ironically.

With an acknowledging lift of his hand, Thane proceeded to head them in the appropriate direction, Dimity already having departed to take her place at once of those tables set aside for the junior members at the gathering.

'You're seated next to me.' Rachel cast Thane a sparkling smile as soon as they reached the table. 'Egan and Narelle can sit next to David. While you're over there.' She waved Adair to the other side with a dismissive hand. 'Between Jill and Stephanie.'

Adair nodded equably, more than content with the arrangement if the other girl did but know it, although she couldn't help but notice that it conveniently left Rachel seated closest to most of the men.

Thane apparently had other notions, however, and voiced them immediately—much to Adair's despair, and Rachel's evident annoyance. 'No, I've a better idea,' he declared calmly, and either ignoring Rachel's disgruntled look, or totally oblivious to it, followed Adair round the table. 'You move up one, mate.' The suggestion to David was half requested, half directed. And when Stephanie followed suit, he took the seat next to Adair.

'Now, isn't that better?' he murmured in a low, drawling undertone, eyeing her wryly.

'In view of the fact that I had no objections to the original arrangement . . . no!' she didn't hesitate to retort as squashingly as it was possible to do in a necessarily muted tone, and was relieved when Stephanie caught her attention in order to introduce those others at the table that she hadn't yet met.

These proved to be the Bowden brothers, Adam and Jason, and another two members of the Craigmont team that Nannawarra would be competing against in the men's A-grade final.

Nevertheless, no sooner were the introductions completed than Thane promptly carried on from where they had left off by contending softly, 'For someone who's supposedly so unafraid, you sure do favour retreating, don't you, angel?'

Forcing herself to remain cool, Adair allowed a mocking curve to edge across her lips. 'Oh, not retreat, Thane,' she contradicted sweetly. 'Rather... detach!'

'Which is a whole lot safer than becoming involved, hmm?'

'Well, it's certainly more agreeable, I can tell you that!'

'Is it?' The look he gave her set her nerves vibrating like a tensioned bow and quickened her breathing. Abruptly, he smiled lazily—a knowing, masculine smile that had a warm wave of colour suffusing her creamy cheeks. 'Then obviously you haven't become involved with the right person yet.'

'That's—purely conjecture on your part!' she was pushed into asserting recklessly.

'Meaning the man who made you erect all those defences *was* the right one for you?' A goading brow rose.

Adair shook her head flusteredly. 'Meaning...oh, it's none of your damned business, and I wish you'd just leave me alone!' She glared at him rancorously before turning hastily to engage Stephanie in conversation. Although what she actually said she neither knew nor cared, as long as it put a stop to Thane's discomposing comments.

A short time later all the talking ceased as everybody took their seats while the President of the Ashvale club said a few appropriate and welcoming words, then the general chatter resumed as the serving of dinner shortly began.

Drinking only a little of the wine provided, and eating even less of her meal, Adair nevertheless kept her eyes and her attention glued to the food in front of her and allowed the conversation at the table to flow around her as if she wasn't there. As, indeed, she wished she wasn't. It had been sheer foolishness on her part to have permitted Stephanie and Narelle to press her into attending, she sighed dejectedly.

'So how's the arm now, Jill?' One particular question from Adam Bowden did succeed in having Adair glancing curiously towards that girl. Had Jill been hurt, then, in one of the later matches of the day that she hadn't stayed to watch?

'Oh, not too bad,' Jill replied lightly, drawing back a long chiffon sleeve to display the bandage wrapping her forearm. 'No thanks to Henry here, though!' She sent a rueful, laughing look towards the man next to her.

'Ah, well . . . when you come up against a better team . . .'

'Better team!' David immediately scoffed in the same bantering manner, taking up the obvious challenge. 'Nannawarra only *let* Craigmont's mixed team win today!'

'Mmm . . . because they couldn't stop them!' put in Jason with a laugh. He leant back in his chair with a goading expression on his pleasant face. 'The same as *your* team won't be able to stop us doing the same to you in the finals tomorrow!'

Not unexpectedly, that remark brought forth even more raillery, from almost everyone at the table, and Adair listened with a strange feeling of loneliness overtaking her. Not that there was anything

she could add to the conversation, even if she had
wanted to, she realised. She really knew very little
about most of the people present, and even less
about polocrosse, especially when their talk became
sprinkled with references to other carnivals, and
other years. Their world, including the outback way
of life led by the majority of those at the table, was
totally alien to her, and so she supposed it would
always remain.

'Perhaps you'd care to dance? That may at least
make the evening seem to disappear more quickly
for you,' Thane put forward suddenly, sardonically, evidently mistakenly attributing her pensive
demeanour to something else entirely.

Until then, Adair hadn't been aware that the
dancing had even begun, but on looking about her
she saw that quite a number of people were already
on the dance floor. Still she shook her head.

'No, thank you,' she declined on a coolly polite
note, remembering all too vividly, among other
things, the last time they had danced. 'I don't feel
in the mood.'

'For dancing at all . . . or just with me?'

'For dancing at all,' she advised in the same flat
vein, and flicked him a speaking glance. 'So instead of wasting your time with me, why don't you
go and ask Rachel? I'm sure you'll find her only
too willing to accept, and her company far more—
gratifying.' A touch of sarcasm surfaced.

Fleetingly, the contours of Thane's face altered,
becoming hard and taut, then they relaxed again as
he rose swiftly upright, his mouth assuming an indifferent curve. 'You're probably right,' he acceded,
and promptly set off for the other side of the table.

Adair watched him with her teeth worrying at her lower lip, surprised by his sudden acquiescence to her rebuff, and inexplicably feeling just a little niggled by the look of sheer self-satisfaction that was evident on Rachel's face when Thane escorted her on to the dance floor.

After having so often demanded that he leave her alone, now that he had, she should have been feeling pleased and relieved, but somehow that didn't appear to be quite the case. Instead, she felt closer to being—deserted? No, that couldn't be, she tried to tell herself with a vexed shake of her head, but the feeling remained despite all her efforts to dispel it.

It couldn't possibly have been that she had just become so accustomed to him disregarding her attempted rejections that she had automatically assumed he would do the same this time too, could it? the alarming surmise followed. Adair swallowed in dismay at the thought. But she didn't *want* him paying her any attention! She couldn't! Abruptly, her vision became misty, and she blinked rapidly to force back all signs of such weakness.

Oh, he was just making her so confused she hardly knew what to think any more! she railed plaintively, and, making hasty excuses to those still left at the table—others also having joined in the dancing by now—she headed for the sanctuary of the relative peace and solitude of the beer garden. Away from the pitying glances she was sure must be coming her way for having been so summarily abandoned, and away from the social gathering she had never really wanted to attend in the first place.

Outside, the air struck chill against Adair's skin—
it was winter, after all, even if in such coastal climates that season wasn't usually particularly
severe—and especially after the warmth that had
been generated by the press of people inside. Sup-
pressing a shiver, she ambled aimlessly between the
small tables and past tubs of palms and other
greenery that decorated the area, until coming to
the wrought-iron railing that bounded the dimly lit
garden where she rested her arms on it pensively,
looking to the swimming pool beyond and wondering inconsequentially whether leaves had something against clear expanses of water for, just as
they did with their own pool at the motel, they all
seemed to be dropping with unerring accuracy right
in the middle of the shimmering water.

From inside the sounds of relaxation and enjoyment still reached her, the music changing to a
faster rhythm now, and then a while later back to
a slower one once more. The band was evidently
attempting to please all tastes and ages, she deduced with a faint lift to her lips.

'I thought you might have left the party
altogether until Jason said he remembered you
saying something about coming out here.' Thane's
voice unexpectedly sounded close behind her, both
startling her and making her stiffen before half
turning to face him.

'Yes, I—felt like getting some fresh air,' she responded as steadily as possible.

'But more than that, you'd like to go home,
wouldn't you?'

Oh, how she wished she could! She lifted one
shoulder in a gesture that was neither assenting nor

dissenting. 'Stephanie would probably never speak to me again if I left this early,' she offered with a weak attempt at a wry half-smile.

His mouth tilted lazily and he lifted a hand to toy with the silky strands of her hair. 'Lucky Stephanie, that you obviously value her feelings so highly,' he declared softly.

Adair's throat constricted, her eyes shading to pools of deep blue as they seemed to become locked inescapably with his. 'Sh-she's a good friend,' she just managed to push out shakily, and all too un-nervingly aware of the fingers that were touching the side of her neck now. Oh, God, what sort of a battle of wills was this, when the minute he touched her she didn't appear to have one of her own any more? She swallowed with difficulty and took a step backwards. 'And—and she's no doubt wondering where I am by now, so perhaps I'd better return inside.'

'Except that I suspect Stephanie has someone other than you on her mind at the moment,' Thane contended drily, seeming to move even closer.

Of course—David! She gulped despairingly. 'I—well...I was about to return, anyway.'

'That's not the impression I received.'

Adair flicked the tip of her tongue over her suddenly dry lips and rubbed her hands along her arms as if to warm them. 'Well...it is—getting cold,' she dissembled, beginning to edge past him.

Without warning, he caught hold of one of her hands between both of his, making her jump nervously and staying her intended flight. 'You don't feel cold,' he contradicted and, lifting her hand, laid his firm lips against the tender skin of the inside of her wrist.

The action galvanised Adair into frantic movement as her blood turned to liquid fire, and she made to snatch her hand away. Only she wasn't fast enough, and his grip tightened inexorably. 'Don't do that!' she flared, quivering. 'I—I want to go inside, Thane!'

His eyes roamed her flushed features slowly, disturbingly. 'In order to join the dancing?'

She nodded jerkily, willing now to consider anything that would just bring them into contact with others. Alone with him like this, she simply felt too unaccountably defenceless.

'We can do that here,' Thane proposed, to her dismay, and drew her into his arms before she could stop him. 'And have the floor all to ourselves.'

Held firmly against his muscular form, the strong arms encircling her making escape impossible, Adair had no choice but to keep in step when he started moving in time to the music coming from the dining-room, her every thought and emotion in chaos.

Her breathing was shallow, her heart racing, her every nerve taut. Although not with apprehension as she initially believed, but seemingly with a tantalising excitement she was at a loss to understand. With her hands trapped against his broad chest, she tried to concentrate on pushing him away, but her senses showed a traitorous tendency to only respond to other stimulations. Such as the hard, muscled flesh she could feel so easily beneath the thin covering of his shirt, the flexing of his powerful legs where they pressed against hers, the clean masculine fragrance of him, the stirring warmth of his breath against her temple.

Then she suddenly remembered the pain and disillusion from when last she had unthinkingly allowed her emotions to rule instead of her mind, *and* the fact that this was merely a challenging weekend interlude for Thane—and amusing egobooster for his prowess with the opposite sex, no doubt!—and she pushed back distractedly against the arms enfolding her, her face tilting upwards.

'Stop *stalking* me, Thane!' she half ordered, half choked, but to her to consternation it sounded more like an entreaty than a castigation, made worse when anguished tears welled unbidden into her eyes.

Although he brought them to a standstill, he didn't release her, but lowered his head instead, his mouth brushing the sensitive area just beneath her ear and then gliding sensuously down the side of her throat, the tip of his tongue tormenting with devastating effect the already throbbing cord it traced downwards.

'I wouldn't have to, if you'd just stop denying your own instincts,' he murmured against her soft skin.

Trembling with shock at the unbridled sensations unexpectedly surging within her, and with her legs feeling as if they were wilting, Adair could only shake her head weakly. 'I'm not—denying them,' she declared on a tremulous note. 'You're just saying that because it suits you to believe it.'

Thane lifted his head, his grey eyes dark as they connected with hers. 'Am I?' he countered in disarmingly lazy tones, and before she had time to answer, his lips claimed hers in a long, drugging kiss that made her heart pound.

Dazed, she struggled feebly against him, a small inarticulate sound issuing from her throat as she felt her resistance waywardly disintegrating and a strange ache starting to spread through her. As if of their own volition, her lips parted, and his tongue slipped between them with a sensuous insistence that left her gasping, and had her hands reaching up to clasp tightly about his strong neck.

He was arousing, and with such consummate ease, emotions she had long thought buried—if indeed Rolfe had ever managed to stimulate such overwhelming feelings as these!—and she could only cling to him helplessly, waiting for the storm to pass.

Then slowly Thane's arms loosened, his hands sliding upwards to weave within the bright coils of her hair, cupping her head, his lips relinquishing hers unhurriedly. 'So you don't deny any such instincts, do you?' he drawled, but with a noticeably husky nuance to his voice.

Self-conscious colour tinged Adair's skin and she pulled free of his hands, turning away from him. 'OK, so you've succeeded in proving that I—I do have—such feelings,' she conceded painfully. Wasn't it enough that he had succeeded in his intent—and to such a demolishing degree—without mocking her for it, too? She sucked in a deep breath. 'However, despite what you're undoubtedly thinking...'

'In which regard *I* sincerely doubt you would even have so much as a clue!' he cut in on a peculiarly rough note.

She slanted him a dubious glance over her shoulder. 'I—well, it's obvious, isn't it?'

'Is it?' Thane spun her back towards him. 'Why?'

'Because all men's minds work the same way!' she retorted bitterly.

His smoky eyes narrowed. 'The same way as whose? Your ex-fiancé's?'

Adair's stomach lurched, and her eyes widened. 'Wh-who told you I'd been engaged?' she queried jerkily.

'Dimity. While I was waiting for you and Narelle she just happened to mention that this evening was the first time anyone—I presumed, of the male persuasion—had called for you since you and your fiancé split up.'

Adair bent her head. 'Well, she shouldn't have!' she protested throatily.

'Because you blame yourself for him jilting you?' Thane demanded in suddenly harsh tones.

Dear God, he knew that was how it had ended too? Her head jerked up again, waves of even deeper colour staining her cheeks now. 'No, I don't blame myself!' She paused, her blue eyes flashing with an acrimonious light. 'But just how long did it take you to prise that piece of information from her?'

'As it happens, I didn't *prise* anything from her!' he denied grimly. 'I merely asked a question—quite absently, as a matter of fact—about your ex-fiancé, and she volunteered the whole story in return.' His features grew sardonic. 'Your niece simply happens to be a damn sight more candid than you, that's all!'

'Evidently!' she seethed, but not game to enquire exactly what the whole story entailed.
'Although none of which has anything to do with
you, in any case!'

'Not even when I'm accused of being in the same
mould as...Rolfe, wasn't it?' He raised such an
expressive brow that Adair's fingers curled into im-
potent fists at her sides.

She didn't bother to dignify his facetiously made
question with a reply, but promptly blazed, 'Then
if you don't care for the comparison, perhaps you
should take the hint and...stop intruding in my
life!'

'Thereby conveniently leaving you to wallow in
your self-pity once more? Uh-uh!' He shook his
head in veto, and suddenly gave a slow smile that,
in spite of everything, still stirred her senses.
'You've got a lot to learn about me, haven't you?'

'Regardless of the fact that I've absolutely no
desire to, apparently!' Adair snipped tartly, breasts
heaving. God, hadn't she come to know too much
about him, and the effect he could have on her,
already? 'And nor do I wallow in self-pity!'

'Hmm...' Thane eyed her consideringly, then
caught her completely off guard by abruptly suggesting, 'Have you ever considered that he might
actually have done you a favour by jilting you?'

Her lips levelled. 'No, I can't say I have! *Favours*
of that kind I think I'd rather give a miss!'

'Although it would have hit even harder, surely,
if you'd married...and *then* he'd shot through,'
he put forward watchfully.

Adair's forehead creased in a frown. Would that
have been a possibility? She wouldn't have thought

so once, but now...? She sighed and returned her attention to the man who was causing all her present problems.

'Yes, well, if it's despicable enough, I guess we can expect it of any male, at that, can't we?' she gibed with a tartly mocking smile, and, elevating her slender nose in dismissal, she turned determinedly for the dining-room.

# CHAPTER FIVE

STEPHANIE arrived in whirlwind fashion the next morning, even before Adair had finished cooking all the breakfasts, Narelle and Dimity already having had theirs and left to attend to their horses.

'Ah, there you are!' she smiled, locating Adair in the kitchen. 'Narelle just asked me to slip across to impress on you not to be late this morning. The second round competition for beaten teams gets under way at eight-thirty and then the finals start at ten.'

'But I had so much time off yesterday...' Adair evaded uncomfortably. She didn't want to disappoint either her sister or her niece, but simultaneously she had no wish to spend any more time than she could avoid in Thane Callahan's increasingly perturbing presence either.

Stephanie immediately cast her an askance gaze. 'And you also know very well your mother said it was quite OK for you to do so,' she charged. 'Besides, these could be their most important matches and they're obviously expecting you to watch them.'

Adair bit her lip contritely. 'It's their last games this morning?' she queried.

'They are if they don't win,' Stephanie replied, her expression turning dry. 'But they're the first matches.' Her glance connected with Adair's unwaveringly.

Adair nodded, her mind racing. If neither Narelle's nor Dimity's team won, she could be back at the motel before the finals started. Of course, if they did... She pushed the thought aside—she would deal with that if and when it occurred—and gave the other girl a smile. 'Then I guess you'd better assure them I'll be there.'

'I should hope so!' her friend mock-censured. About to depart, she looked back part curiously, part diffidently. 'So what did you think of the dinner dance last night? I thought you looked as if you found it...not quite as unenjoyable as you anticipated.'

Because she hadn't been permitted *not* to join in the dancing? When the words she and Thane had exchanged had appeared to be casual conversation, but most of the time had, in actual fact, been verbal sparring? Adair recalled with a grimace.

'Yes—well, it was certainly—different—from what I'd been expecting,' she owned, ironically, but not wanting to hurt the other girl's feelings by saying she would far rather not have gone.

'I'm glad.' Stephanie smiled her relief, and her brown eyes began to twinkle with a teasing light. 'You see, I told you you'd change your mind once you got to know some of our male visitors, didn't I?' And with a delighted chuckle she hurried on her way, leaving Adair to make a disgruntled moue in her wake.

Not for quite the reason Stephanie apparently believed, but oh, yes, there had definitely been changes in her mind! she had to concede. But, dismayingly, from detached, unruffled control to distinct awareness and unsettled discomposure! Her only sustaining thought was that after the next few days she would, thank goodness, never see Thane Callahan again! Well, not until next year at least, she amended with a sigh.

Yet again for Narelle's and Dimity's sakes, Adair ensured that she arrived at the grounds in plenty of time to see their two teams take to their respective fields. However, it wasn't until she joined the expanding crowd preparing to view the opening matches that it began to register on her just how many red and grey-shirted forms there were already among the crowd. But Nannawarra's teams weren't due to compete until the finals, she frowned, then abruptly closed her eyes in despair on remembering. Except for their mixed team which Craigmont had defeated yesterday! she now recalled. How could she have forgotten?

'Hi! Have you come to see if Rachel and Jill and the rest of our mixed team can do better at upholding our club's honour this morning than they did yesterday?' David's cheerful voice suddenly questioned beside her, containing all the bantering superiority of one who was a member of their so far successful men's A-team.

A hasty glance round showed him to be alone, and Adair relaxed a little as she shook her head. 'Sorry, but I'm here to watch Narelle and Dimity play, actually.'

David nodded understandingly. 'Well, we'll see you again later, anyway, I expect. We're playing on one of the other fields, so I guess I'd better go and lend my support... as well as a few words of evidently required advice,' he grinned, turning to leave. 'I'll let Thane know you're here.'

'No!' she protested, aghast, and unsure why he should consider Thane ought to be told anyway. At his surprised look for her vehemence, she forced a smile on to her lips and continued in a markedly more moderate tone, 'No, don't bother. Since the Ashvale games seem likely to finish first...' both of them were on the field now and starting to line up, whereas Nannawarra and their opponents were only just approaching their field of play '...I expect I'll—er—wander over to see the conclusion of your match, in any case.'

'OK.' He accepted her explanation equably, and continued on his way, while Adair heaved a sigh of relief and tried to concentrate her attention on the contests taking place in front of her.

That none of the teams was quite to the standard displayed by some of the others the day before soon became obvious, but even so it also became clear that her sister's team, at least, were going to be the eventual winners, and Adair's heart sank. She was pleased for Narelle, naturally enough, but how could she leave now? Having won that particular match meant her sister was through to the beaten teams' final in their division, and she strongly suspected there was just no way Narelle would countenance her missing her participation in *that* event!

As a result, she was more or less resigned to, if not in accord with, meeting Thane some time during the day, although still not fully prepared for that encounter to occur even before the conclusion of the games she was watching. Her first intimation of his presence came a few minutes before the bells

signalling the end of the final chukkas, when a
muscular arm was suddenly draped loosely across
her shoulders.

'I thought I might find you here,' Thane said
idly. 'So how are they doing?' with a nod towards
the appropriate fields.

'Oh—er—Dimity's going to lose, but Narelle's
through to the final,' faltered Adair, profoundly
aware of both his touch and the hard male form in
such close contact with hers due to the press of the
crowd. She swallowed and spared him a brief
glance. 'And—and Nannawarra? I thought you'd
be watching their game.'

'I have been, but as the outcome is already
beyond doubt...' He shrugged and cast her a
leisurely look that had her throat constricting. 'I
decided it was time to look for you...' he paused,
a wry curve caught at the edges of his well-shaped
mouth '...before you probably disappeared for the
day.'

Adair moistened her lips, fighting for control of
her errantly floundering senses. 'You're very per-
sistent,' she attempted to protest, but her voice was
too husky to convey the asperity she wanted to
project.

'I was about to say the same of you,' Thane returned as he wound his fingers significantly within
the strands of the hair that she had automatically
tied back again so tightly that morning.

Surmising exactly what would be happening next,
Adair exhaled a partly aggrieved, partly resigned
breath and reached up to dispose of the confining
rubber band herself. 'All right?' A faintly gibing
note emerged as she shook her hair free.

He inclined his head fractionally, his expression whimsical as he went on to muse, 'I wonder if you would eventually also be so accommodating if, in an attempt to improve your unflattering mode of dress as well,' he plucked at the ill-fitting olive-coloured blouse she was wearing loose over a too-bulky skirt, 'I started removing those every time you stubbornly insisted on wearing them?'

Although it was said in a dry and purely conjectural manner, Adair was shocked to discover her ensuing thoughts were anything but! Instead, she found herself incomprehensibly speculating just what it would be like to be undressed by Thane Callahan, to feel those hard hands of his caressing her bare skin, to surrender herself to him completely. Then sanity returned with a gasp, her face crimsoning at the alarming meanderings of her mind, and she bent her head so that her hair fell forward to cover her flaming cheeks protectively.

'Since it—it's never likely to happen, it seems... doubtful,' she all but mumbled.

'But an... evocative notion, none the less,' Thane lowered his head to murmur expressively, and had her composure splintering even further. There was a slight pause before he continued. 'So how would you suggest I go about achieving such a result?'

More flustered than she would have believed, she impulsively said the first thing that came to mind. 'Why should you care... or—or want to?'

The fingers resting against her shoulder tightened imperceptibly. 'Why do you think?'

Adair ventured a swift look upwards from the cover of long, glossy lashes. 'Because you see it as an...amusing challenge, I suppose,' she hazarded flatly.

'Well, I'll give you, it's certainly a challenge,' Thane owned, the corners of his mouth abruptly quirking with dry humour. 'But—amusing...?' He shook his head slowly, his hand beginning to stroke the side of her neck softly, and when he continued his tone seemed to have deepened somehow. 'No, amusement has never been on my mind where you're concerned.'

Adair's breath quickened. She felt as if her last vestige of willpower was being drained from her, and made a supreme effort to retain what little was left. 'But as I've already said...' She halted as a burst of clapping broke out around them, signifying the end of the match, and she hastily made the most of the opportunity it provided to escape by going on to exclaim, 'Oh, I must go and congratulate Narelle!'

'While I'd better do the same to our team,' he declared, but without releasing her when she would have begun moving away. Instead, he half turned her back towards him, his grey eyes intent as they connected with hers. 'Will you be staying for her final?'

For a moment she was tempted to lie, then discounted the idea and gave an affirming nod.

'For the others too?'

Her heart jumped. 'You—want me to?' The almost whispered question tumbled out before she was really aware of it even forming.

'Would I have asked, if I didn't?' he countered almost as softly.

Adair shook her head weakly, wondering what on earth had prompted her into making such an unthinking query. 'I haven't changed my mind, Thane...about anything,' she averred in an effort to regain lost ground.

'Nor have I,' he contended in suddenly throaty tones, and dropped a kiss on to her unsuspecting and parted lips.

*'Thane!'* she immediately half remonstrated, half pleaded, flushing once more, but too self-conscious to even look round to see if anyone had witnessed the incident that was the cause of her heart's present wild beating.

His white teeth flashed in a rakish and utterly unrepentant smile that promptly had her legs feeling distinctly rubbery as well. 'But you will stay?' he pressed persuasively.

Adair eyed him helplessly. 'Oh, I guess so.' Dear God, when he looked at her like that she seemed to have no wish to refuse him anything!

'That's my girl!' He grazed her cheek gently with the knuckles of one hand, his expression sobering slightly. 'And I'll see you at lunch, if I don't see you again beforehand?'

Was there any point in refusing? Or, at the moment, did she even want to, if it came to that? She nodded her acquiescence, and with another captivating smile in acknowledgement Thane finally removed his arm from about her shoulders and took his departure.

With that removal, however, Adair experienced an odd sense of loss, but only to feel equally strangely compensated by his earlier casually proprietorial remark, it appeared. And for a time she contemplated musingly just what it would be like to be Thane's girl. At least, that was until she realised exactly what she was doing and caught herself up with a gulp and a flurry of self-censure.

With the eventual completion of the second round competition, everyone's attention focused on the longer, six-chukka finals, Narelle's team becoming runners-up in their grade, but Nannawarra's team winning theirs in convincing fashion, not surprisingly, since they had been expected to gain a place in the first round final.

It then became a question of whether the two Nannawarra men's teams were going to continue the pattern. A subject that attracted much discussion during the lunch break, and not only from the club's members and supporters, but also from a great many others present—particularly the A-grade final—because that was always the event that drew the most attention.

'I gather you and Craigmont have been rivals for a long time,' commented Adair impulsively to Thane after Adam Bowden had just made a few more bantering remarks about their team's chances as he passed the area where the Nannawarra camp was congregated.

His lips twitched humorously. 'Mmm, for many years now, and they're very anxious to avenge their defeats of the last three Ashvale carnivals.'

'It's always the two of you who fight out the final?' Her brows drew together a little. That didn't seem fair somehow.

Thane shook his head. 'It's no foregone conclusion, if that's what you're implying,' he corrected in dry tones. 'Particularly if Wuduru also send a team, as they usually do. And neither are any defeats necessarily all in finals, I might add.' He flexed a broad shoulder, his mouth shaping rue-fully. 'If you haven't been able to fit in as much practice as you should, or if your horses aren't quite as fit they could be...' He shrugged again, meaningfully.

Adair nodded and cast him a sideways glance. 'Although you did win last year?'

'Yes. That was the year David came back into the team after having been absent interstate for a couple of years, and he strengthened it considerably.'

Curiosity got the better of her and her head tilted to one side. 'And do you and David play in the same—section? I couldn't tell yesterday, with you wearing helmets.' Which was funny really, she mused, because although she hadn't been able to distinguish David, she'd had no trouble at all in detecting Thane, even when unable to see the number on his shirt.

'No, he's best in attack, the same position I play, so he's part of the other section,' she was advised.

'And is he better than you, or are you better than he is?' Adair ventured to quiz, tongue in cheek.

Thane's mouth shaped crookedly, his eyes con-taining an implicit glint that sent a shiver of vi-carious excitement chasing down her spine. 'As to that, I guess it will be up to you to judge,' he pro-posed lazily.

Refusing to be outfaced—again!—Adair re-turned his gaze valiantly. 'I'll look forward to it,' she quipped.

He gave a low vibrant laugh. 'While supporting...which team?'

The abrupt change of topic caught her unawares. 'I—why, what makes you think I'll be supporting either of you?' she parried.

Thane shrugged negligently. 'Stephanie, Narelle, and Dimity will be.'

She didn't need to ask which team. 'Then maybe I should support Craigmont...in order to at least try and even things up, as it were,' she suggested flippantly, rallying.

'You probably would, at that,' he allowed in a roughening drawl.

Adair caught her lip between shining white teeth, her fingers toying absently with the empty fruit juice bottle on the table in front of them. For some unknown reason she somehow felt guilty all of a sudden. 'You should know that if—if I support anyone...it will be Nannawarra,' she confessed uncomfortably on a low note.

'Should I?'

She made an indecisive gesture. 'Well, I don't really know any of the Craigmont players that well.'

'With your outlook, I would have thought you'd consider that a point in their favour,' he mocked.

'The more so as each minute passes, I'm beginning to think!' she was nettled into sniping in response.

'Meaning...?'

Adair pressed her lips together vexedly. 'Meaning, it would be no more than you deserve if I *did* support Craigmont!' she huffed, but in such a revealing tone of resignation that they both knew she wouldn't be, and she turned her head away in a suddenly irritated movement.

Damn, damn, damn! Why did she allow him to unsettle her to such a degree that she always seemed to end up doing exactly as he wanted?

All such perturbing thoughts were forgotten by the time the A-grade final got under way, however. The preceding games, deciding the winners of the lower grades, had already created a great deal of excitement and stimulated everyone's interest.

Nevertheless, Adair still wasn't prepared for the feeling of tense expectation that gripped her immediately Nannawarra and Craigmont took to the field, nor for the inexplicably fervent desire for Thane's team to succeed. Why should it matter to her which of them won? Probably only because she was standing with her sister and niece, as well as Stephanie—whose loyalties were unmistakable— and it was proving infectious, she dismissed off-handedly, and gave herself up to concentrating on the play that had just begun.

It soon became apparent that there was little between the two teams and, not unexpectedly, that it would be the hardest game contested during the whole carnival. Adair's heart seemed to be continually in her mouth as riders and horses wheeled and swerved with unbelievable speed, slid to halts, and thundered up and down the field, pairs of them often locked together in tenacious physical battles to force an opponent away from the ball or over the sidelines.

Despite Nannawarra's early lead, by the half-time bell the teams were even again, the two succeeding chukkas proving to be see-sawing affairs as first one side and then the other gained the upper hand, so that it wasn't until the final chukka that the outcome was decided. This appeared to be a test of fitness and endurance, but although the pace and the pressure were obviously beginning to tell on all the players and their mounts, in the end it was the evidently fitter and more powerful Nannawarra combination that prevailed, and when Thane scored the final goal just on the bell, giving them a score of fifteen to twelve, a jubilant cheer erupted from the team's many supporters.

'They won, they won!' Dimity couldn't keep from jumping up and down in her excitement, and was equally exuberant throughout the customary photo-taking and trophy presentations that followed.

There were also awards for individual players in various categories, as well as one for the best horse, Adair discovered, Thane securing both the best horse award and the trophy for the best Number One player at the carnival. The judges' decision concerning the latter definitely settled any dispute regarding whether he or David was the best in the attack position, Adair conceded wryly. Or it would have, if she hadn't already secretly come to the same conclusion herself.

With the presentation finalised, the crowd began to disperse, some to make ready for the trip home, some to partake of refreshments, and many others, like Dimity and Narelle, heading for the horse stalls in order to offer either their compliments or condolences to the participants in the last game.

'You're coming too, aren't you?' her niece asked Adair as they were about to set off.

'Yes, of course she is.' It was Stephanie who spoke up swiftly when it seemed a refusal was forthcoming, beaming engagingly as her friend started propelling her along with them.

Adair sighed and cast the other girl a speaking glance. 'I think the only reason you keep insisting I stay around is in order to make your own besotted pursuit of David a little less obvious!' she charged drily in a whisper.

'Now would I really do something like that?' countered Stephanie, trying unsuccessfully to keep a straight face.

'Yes!' Adair had no compunction in asserting ruefully, and they both laughed.

When they arrived at the stalls there seemed to be a mass of people already present. Egan Callahan, together with Jill and Rachel; the other team members' families; as well as many of the club's general supporters who loyally followed them to all carnivals. But although her three companions happily joined the elated throng, Adair hung back self-consciously. For a number of reasons she felt out of place, not the least being that she didn't want Thane to think that the decision to come had been hers.

Consequently, it wasn't until many of the others had eventually drifted away that Thane, in particular, realised she was even present, but in spite of her actually preferring it that way, when he didn't immediately make a move towards her or beckon her over she knew a moment's surprise—and disappointment. The feeling was so unexpected, and so disquieting, that in the hope that some conversation might dispel it, she promptly turned and headed for the washdown area where David, with Stephanie in attendance, was hosing his mount. Since congratulations did seem to be in order, she would as soon give them to him anyway, she decided.

'Mmm, it was a good match, wasn't it?' David agreed after acknowledging her opening remarks with a smile, and continuing to play the water over the big brown gelding which seemed to be thoroughly enjoying the treatment. 'You can bet your boots Craigmont will be out to turn the tables on us the next carnival we both attend.'

Adair considered it more than probable. 'And when is that likely to be?'

'Oh, in about three weeks, I think,' he advised casually. 'Wuduru have their carnival then. Luckily, it's in our own zone, though, so we won't have quite so far to travel.' He gave a resigned hunch, his mouth curving ruefully. 'It's going to be a long trip home tonight with all the horses.'

'You're leaving tonight?' Her eyes widened.

Stephanie's doleful nod was sufficient answer, even without his confirming, 'Uh-huh! It's only Egan and Thane...oh, and Rachel now, too, who are staying on for a few days.'

Adair nodded. 'I see.' It was the first she had heard of the other girl remaining in Ashvale, and momentarily she was beset by the unaccountable temptation to claim that the motel didn't have a vacancy for his sister, but dismissed it vexedly. What did it matter to her whether Rachel stayed or not?

Meanwhile, having turned off the hose, David led his mount from the concreted area and looped an arm about Stephanie's shoulders. 'So in case I don't happen to see you again before we leave, I guess I'd better say goodbye. At least, until next year,' he added with a smile.

'When I hope to see that you're still in one piece,' Adair surprised herself by smiling in return. 'Because you're all quite mad the way you ride those horses, you know that, don't you?'

He grinned broadly, his gaze going past her to Thane as he also came to hose his horse down. 'She thinks we're mad,' he relayed to the other man before inclining his head in a salute to Adair and, with Stephanie accompanying him, continued on his way.

Meanwhile, Thane didn't immediately turn the hose on, but remained beside her, his gaze quizzical as he surveyed her now almost defiant expression. 'Why mad?' he queried watchfully.

'Because you could have broken your stupid necks out there! Or—or injured your horses!' she appended rapidly, not wanting him to think her concern had been for himself. 'It was downright dangerous!'

'No, it wasn't, otherwise the umpire would have awarded penalties. It was simply hard riding, that's all.' He paused, his own demeanour hardening a little. 'In any event, why would you have cared if we had come to grief? You weren't exactly eager to join us afterwards, were you? For a time, I didn't even think you intended coming at all, in fact.'

Adair thrust her hands into the big pockets in her skirt and gave an indifferent shrug. 'Then you were wrong, weren't you? Not that you seemed to care that I had, anyway! Even when you did see me, you made it plain you weren't interested in hearing if I had anything to say!' she accused on a noticeably reproachful note that had her abruptly gulping in dismay. It made it sound as if she considered she had a right to his attention!

An oblique half-smile touched the corners of Thane's lips, and he laid his free hand against the nape of her neck, urging her nearer. 'I wasn't at the time ... while Rachel was so busily yapping in my ear!'

'Oh!' She averted her gaze self-consciously, aware of a disconcerting flicker of pleasure inside her. She was also close enough to be very much conscious of the warm male scent of him, the distinctive smell of horses and polished leather that enveloped them. The combination stirred her senses with a vague excitement and she moved out of reach rapidly, restively. 'I—well, congratulations on your win, anyway,' she just managed to push out with some semblance of equanimity.

Thane inclined his head in lazy acknowledgement, leading his mount on to the concrete now to begin spraying water over the sleek-coated, powerfully built chestnut, thereby reminding Adair of the animal's part in the proceedings.

'And—and for taking out the trophy for best horse, of course,' she added diffidently. As if knowing he was being spoken about, the big gelding tossed his head proudly and a brief half-smile touched Adair's lips before she continued in an almost shy vein, 'He's very beautiful.' She paused. 'What do you call him?'

'Trojan,' Thane supplied. 'And he certainly worked well out there this afternoon. Didn't you, feller?' He gave the horse a couple of solid pats on the neck that had the gelding nudging him in the chest with its head in return.

Adair watched them contemplatively, knowing she should take the opportunity to leave, but seemingly reluctant to do so. 'You use him for stock work when you're at home, I suppose,' she hazarded.

'As much as possible,' he agreed. 'With the cattle, especially. It's good practice.'

'Cattle...especially?' she queried, her brow furrowing.

'Uh-huh!' He turned to eye her humorously. 'We run sheep, in the main.'

'Oh, I didn't realise,' she mumbled, flushing. Not that there was any way she could have known, she excused herself, even if it was a widely recognised fact that the Nannawarra district had always been known primarily as sheep country. 'I—er—just assumed, from the manner in which your horses lean into and—and push between the opposition so fearlessly, that they must have been more practised in working with cattle.' Purposely not affording him any chance to reply, she went on, 'But now I guess it's time I was leaving. I'll have to start setting the tables in the restaurant shortly.' The uneasy moment had spurred her into making a move at least—and at last, she was relieved to note.

Finished with the hose, Thane turned it off and nodded slowly, as if acknowledging that she did have some responsibilities that just couldn't be discounted. 'Although you'll join us for a celebratory drink later this evening.' It was more of a statement than a question.

'Us?' Adair queried curiously before she could stop herself.

Thane shrugged as he drew level with her. 'Those members of our teams—plus wives or girlfriends, etcetera—and a few of the others who also intend remaining overnight.'

She shook her head in refusal. 'I doubt if I'll be finished in time.'

'Not even by ten-thirty...on a Sunday?' He crooked a chafingly sceptical brow.

In view of the restaurant mainly being provided as a convenience for travelling guests, who normally weren't interested in dining until the late hours, it was usually well and truly closed and the kitchen thoroughly cleaned as well by ten-thirty on any day, but Adair was reluctant to admit as much.

'Well, even if it was tonight...' she hedged, 'I can't imagine I'd feel like tramping all the way over here again at that time of night.'

'That shouldn't present any problem, then, because we normally have it in one of our rooms at the motel,' he declared drily, unexpectedly totally destroying that argument.

'Oh!' Her fingers curled and uncurled restlessly within the deep pockets of her skirt. 'Well, I hope it won't be a—a noisy celebration, because there are other guests who'll be wishing to sleep, you know,' she reminded him in her most prim manner, deliberately veering from the main subject.

'Mmm, we do realise that,' drawled Thane. 'However, we appear to have digressed...' He eyed her implicitly.

So much for attempting to change the topic, sighed Adair, wondering why she didn't just refuse outright. Probably because she had tried that tack before—quite unsuccessfully!—she recalled with a grimace.

'Yes, well, I'm afraid the best I can promise is that I'll come if I possibly can,' she proposed, but without actually intending to do anything of the kind. 'Now, I really must go. I'm late already.' She was on her way before she had even finished speaking.

'And I'll ensure that you keep to that!' Thane called after her smoothly.

Adair cast a frowning glance over her shoulder, but didn't stop moving, and with a dismissive toss of her long hair she continued on to the motel.

# CHAPTER SIX

As IT so happened, Adair finished her tasks in the restaurant and kitchen some time before ten that evening, and was happily congratulating herself on the thought that she would be in bed and asleep before Thane even returned to the motel when her mother caught at her arm as they headed for their own quarters.

'Oh, do go and check for me to see if there are any late breakfast menus in the box outside the office, Adair,' Gemma Newman requested. 'I meant to look earlier, but then it completely slipped my mind.'

'That's OK, it's no trouble,' Adair smiled easily, already changing direction and making for the door that gave on to the courtyard.

Outside, the air was crystal-clear, the stars brilliant against their inky backdrop, and she rounded the corner of the office with a light step, although only to have her pace slow markedly on seeing the lights aglow in two particular units opposite, and from one of which came the hum of conversation, interspersed with the clink of glassware and the sudden rumble of quiet mirth. So their celebration was already under way, Adair mused in surprise as she absently extracted the three late orders for breakfast from the box provided.

As she was about to swiftly retrace her steps, one of the doors was abruptly opened to spill strong light into the courtyard, catching Adair directly in its beam, and Egan Callahan emerged before she could disappear back around the corner.

'Hello, Adair,' he greeted her warmly. 'You're on your way to join us for a drink too, are you? Is Narelle with you?'

'Narelle?' she repeated blankly in confusion.

'Yes, she said she'd be coming over once the work in the restaurant was finished.'

'Oh, I didn't know,' she said lamely, moving restlessly from one foot to the other. She didn't want to stand there talking. She just wanted to disappear—before someone next door perhaps overheard and came to see what was happening!

'Well, never mind, I expect she'll be along in a minute or two,' Egan Callahan went on in the same friendly fashion. 'The two of us may as well join the party while we're waiting, though.' Already he was making a move to grasp the handle of the appropriate door.

'Oh, but I can't...!' Adair began frantically, only to stop on hearing the door of another unit slam, and to see Rachel—dressed to the nines in elegant green silk—approaching at the same as Narelle now arrived on the scene.

'Well, it seems we all have the same destination in mind,' laughed Narelle as she headed across the courtyard to join Egan Callahan and Rachel. But seeing her sister hadn't followed her, she turned back to exhort humorously, 'Come on, Adair, the party's inside, not out here!'

Notwithstanding, Adair remained exactly where she was. 'Except that I...'

'Oh, for heaven's sake! I came to take part in a celebration, not a dissertation!' cut in Rachel impatiently, her voice sounding doubly loud in the clear night air. 'You can stay out here talking all you want, but *I'm* going inside!' She stepped forward to fling open the door to Thane's unit with a determined flourish.

Adair could quite cheerfully have choked her. Twice, in fact, if that could have been possible, when her worst fears were immediately realised and her heart plummeted to somewhere in the vicinity of her knees when Thane himself promptly appeared in the doorway.

'Are you planning on holding your own party out here?' he enquired of his father in a wry drawl, rapidly scanning those present.

Across the courtyard, Adair debated whether she could feasibly disappear while they were talking, but Egan Callahan unknowingly put paid to that idea.

'No, we simply all arrived at much the same time, that's all,' he explained with a laugh. 'We were just about to join you, as a matter of fact.'

For her part, Adair waved the breakfast orders in her hand distractedly and promptly tried to dispute once more, 'No—actually—I was just . . .'

'Mmm, you were just . . . ?' Thane raised a provoking brow as he began pacing towards her, while the others—Rachel conversely reluctant now—entered the room behind him.

She drew a slightly ragged breath and held the papers more firmly. 'I was collecting these . . . in—in order to take them back to the kitchen,' she added as a hasty afterthought.

'Although I doubt they'll be missed if they make a detour for a while,' he put forward on a confident note and, linking his arm with hers, determinedly started back for the unit with her in tow.

'But—but . . .' Adair spluttered indignantly, then heaved a disgruntled sigh and resigned herself to the inevitable. Oh, what the hell! she grimaced. There were hardly likely to be any disturbing incidences with so many others present, including his father and her own sister, and she could always leave when everyone else did.

Which was precisely what she did some one and a half hours later, after an unexpectedly pleasant time among a sociable—well, apart from Rachel for the most part, that was—and often amusing group of people, not all of them from the Nannawarra district, but obviously good friends none the less, who had crowded into the unit to sprawl over the beds, chairs, the floor, and anywhere else that provided a patch of space.

However, no sooner had Adair reached her own room than she clamped a hand on her mouth in dismay. The breakfast orders! She had put them down somewhere in Thane's unit, and forgotten all about them when she left. Briefly, she was tempted to ignore them altogether, in spite of knowing in her subconscious that just wasn't possible. The people concerned would be expecting their breakfasts in the morning, no matter if she was nervous at the thought of returning for their menu sheets!

But nervous of what? she suddenly demanded of herself. Good lord, the man could hardly ravish her in a motel full of people! Her own family's motel, at that! And where was her own fortitude, anyway?

Or had that now dissolved as completely as had her memory regarding the menus? The nettling suggestion had her standing her tallest in silent denial and resolutely making her way back to Thane's unit.

Rapping forcefully on the door, Adair waited impatiently for it to be opened—it seemed to be taking an inordinate amount of time!—although as soon as it was finally thrown wide, a sizeable portion of her poise promptly slipped considerably.

With his only covering a towel fastened about his lean hips, it was evident Thane had been preparing for bed. Or she might even have roused him from it, Adair speculated discomfitedly, that image somehow triggering even stronger feelings of warm self-consciousness. But she definitely hadn't anticipated being confronted by such an unsettling expanse of darkly tanned skin; or such a broad chest, heavily muscled shoulders and arms; a flat and hard stomach, and long muscular legs.

'And to what do I owe this unexpected pleasure?' enquired Thane lazily. A roguish glint entered his smoky grey eyes. 'Or have you perhaps come to turn down the covers for me?'

'Of c-course not!' Adair's denial had a strangled sound about it. Did he have to exude such an unnerving and dangerously blatant maleness? she despaired inconsequentially. 'I—I forgot the breakfast orders when I left, so I came back for them.'

'In that case, I guess you'd better come in and look for them.' Thane stood aside from the door, and she was profoundly aware of the virile strength of him as his muscles rippled with every easy movement. 'I didn't see them when I tidied up.'

Adair shuffled her feet uneasily, reluctant to actually enter the room. 'I think I put them on the small table beside the bed,' she advised, hoping he would take the hint and do the looking for her.

He shrugged and gestured in the appropriate direction. 'Well, they're not there now...as you can see.' His mouth assumed a mocking cast. 'Or you'd be able to if you stopped hovering around out there like some nervous damn schoolgirl on her first date, and came inside!'

Annoyed with both him and herself, Adair flashed him a baleful glare and stormed into the room to immediately begin searching around the table in question. When that proved fruitless, she looked around with a frown. 'But I was positive that's where I put them.'

Having been leaning negligently against the door jamb, Thane now pushed the door closed and moved further into the room, flexing a wide shoulder with an almost languid grace. 'Maybe someone moved them.'

'I guess they must have done,' she conceded, biting her lip. Then, diffidently, because it *was* his room for the time being, after all, 'Would you mind if I looked round a bit further?'

'Feel free,' he invited drily. 'You won't come across any bodies secreted beneath the beds, or anything of that order, I can assure you.'

Adair flushed involuntarily. Was that why he thought she had been unwilling to enter the room? she wondered. In case he had a female companion for the night? In one way she found the idea relieving, but in another inexplicably depressing, although she staunchly disguised it with a quip.

'They would need to be thin, then, because there's only an inch or so clearance between these ensemble beds and the floor!' She slanted him a sideways glance, something inside her unable to resist gibing, 'Or do you have a partiality for wafer-thin females?'

'That's a leading question, isn't it?' Thane's mouth shaped whimsically, but it was the look in his eyes—unwavering, assessing, dangerously implicit—that had her dropping her gaze first and regretting her impulsiveness.

'Yes, it was,' she owned faintly, and turned to push the bed aside in order to look behind it. 'I'm sorry.'

Thane shook his head wryly and closed the gap between them. 'I'll push—you look,' he instructed laconically.

A half smile of gratitude flickered about the edges of Adair's lips, and doing as directed, she was rewarded by seeing some paper come into view. 'There they are!' she exclaimed and, bending, picked up two forms. Realising the third wasn't with them, she got down on her hands and knees to peer under the bed to see if she could locate it, but to no avail, and she sat back on her heels, frowning. 'There should be another one, though.'

'How about under this one?' Thane helpfully pulled the other bed away from the wall.

Crawling the short distance across to it, she squinted into the shadows beneath the bed while he surveyed the newly revealed floor area. 'It's not here either,' she half sighed, half grimaced.

'Are you sure?' He got down beside her to check for himself.

'Well?' she questioned sardonically when he raised his head again.

'It's not there either,' he allowed with a grin that set the nerves of her stomach quivering. 'So are you positive there even *was* another one?'

Adair nodded shakily. 'Yes, I'm sure there was.' She hesitated, her expression becoming a touch rueful. 'Although I must confess you're making me start to have my doubts.'

'Only about the number of breakfast orders there should be?' Thane's voice slowed and deepened as he reached up one hand to tangle his fingers in the long strands of her hair.

The subtle change in subject and mood had Adair swallowing nervously. 'I don't know what you mean,' she prevaricated on a breathless note, and made to rise to her feet, but an imperceptible pressure on her hair prevented her.

'I think you do,' he contradicted wryly, smoothly. 'For in spite of your early reluctance, you weren't nearly as reserved this evening as you have been previously.' His lips twitched fleetingly. 'Or was that merely due to the vodka and orange you were drinking?'

Adair licked at her lips. She didn't know about it having had an effect on her attitude then, but she definitely suspected it might have been a contributing factor to the feeling of lassitude that had suddenly begun to assail her. 'They were nice people,' she declared weakly.

'Even the males among them?' in gently bantering disbelief.

She shook her head at his teasing tone. 'Even them, I suppose,' she owned grudgingly, albeit with that faint qualification. Putting a hand on the bed, she prepared to make another effort to rise. 'None the less, I still have a breakfast order to locate, and...'

'You can do that after,' Thane interrupted to propose in thickening tones, his hand sliding deeper into her hair to cup the back of her head.

'After?' Widening blue eyes fastened warily to darkening grey.

'Mmm, after...this.' Thane tipped her face up to his, his own head lowering with obvious intent, but she swiftly turned her head away and his lips only found the corner of her soft mouth. But even that less than complete contact she discovered to be profoundly disturbing.

'No! I...'

Her agitated protest was cut short by Thane's firm mouth covering hers fully this time, his other arm wrapping about her slender form to draw her closer. In an effort to prevent him, Adair brought her hands up between them, but as they came to rest against the solid wall of his chest she experienced a sudden, tantalising desire to explore the muscular flesh instead, and her fingers began to smooth upwards tentatively to his broad shoulders.

Thane uttered a muffled groan and the arm encircling her tightened, sweeping her even nearer and lifting her effortlessly as he eased them both on to the bed, his long legs entangling with hers as he leant over her. With deliberate expertise, his lips moved on hers, urgently at first, and then with a tormenting persuasiveness so that almost before Adair knew it she was opening her mouth willingly to his probing, savouring tongue.

Once again he was resurrecting emotions she hadn't ever wanted to feel again—and perhaps even some she hadn't known she possessed! Adair conceded dazedly—but none of which she now seemed capable of controlling. It didn't even appear to matter just how potentially dangerous her situation was, lying on a bed with an as good as naked man, and especially one as ultra-masculine as Thane Callahan. For the moment she only knew her senses welcomed the consuming kisses and the leisurely caresses that were making her limbs grow weak.

Moving slightly, Thane's lips sought the soft curve of her throat, and the palpitating hollow at its base, his tongue slowly brushing the sweetly scented skin, his hand pushing her loose-fitting top and bra strap from her shoulder in order to seek the swelling curves of a rounded breast. Adair trembled at the intimate contact, her breathing becoming ragged as his fingers explored the soft flesh with unhurried indulgence and he bent his head to draw the already hardening nipple into his mouth, his tongue curling and swirling about it sensuously until it peaked tautly, whereupon he began to suck gently.

Shaken to the core of her being as her body responded ungovernably to every arousing touch, Adair wound her arms around his neck, her fingers twining tightly within his thick, dark hair as she moved against him invitingly.

Lifting his head, Thane reclaimed her lips hungrily, his breath warm as it mingled with hers. 'Stay the night with me,' he whispered huskily against the corner of her mouth in a voice heavy with desire. 'I want to make love to you, to sleep

with you in my arms, and...' he touched her skirt
cursorily, 'with none of these restrictions between
us.'

With his words, Adair's pulsebeat slowed and her
wits gradually cleared. Oh, God, if he hadn't
spoken she doubted she would have had the incli-
nation, or the willpower, to refrain from doing precisely as he suggested! she suddenly realised with
an appalled gulp.

'I—I can't,' she declared unsteadily, avoiding his
gaze as she hastily rearranged her clothing. 'And
th-this isn't why I came back here.'

His lips twisted. 'I know that!' Pausing, he
stroked a finger along the underside of her jaw.
'But I also know that a moment ago you weren't
exactly unwilling for me to continue,' he said softly.

Adair couldn't control the colour that washed
into her cheeks. 'No—well...now I am,' she only
just succeeded in getting out jerkily, easing away
from him.

Thane pushed himself up on the pillow, supporting his weight on an elbow. 'Now that you've
remembered I'm one of the enemy...a male?' His
voice roughened fractionally with a thread of
mockery.

Did he really believe she could ever possibly
forget, or ignore, that so essential maleness that
surrounded him? she mused almost hysterically.
Sucking in a deep breath, she shrugged with assumed detachment. 'Look, I'm sorry if your ego
finds it impossible to accept that I'm just not
interested, but...' She broke off apprehensively
when a hard hand abruptly spanned her chin.

'You reckon I couldn't disprove that if I chose to?' he half laughed sardonically.

Alarmed by the implicit threat, Adair wrenched free of his grasp and scrambled from the bed with more haste than grace.

Thane merely eyed her tauntingly from between narrowed lids and gave another mirthless laugh. 'Oh, don't worry, I'm not in the habit of forcing females into sharing my bed,' he mocked.

No, they doubtlessly did so more than willingly! she thought bitterly, and just a little dispiritedly. But she was still embarrassedly aware that her rapid flight had revealed all too plainly her fear of his actually proving how easily he could have overcome her resistance.

In consequence she couldn't continue to hold his gaze, so she averted her own—which chanced upon a slip of paper protruding from behind the pillow she had dislodged in her hurried vacation of the bed, and she pounced on it with heartfelt relief.

'In—in any case, I have to take these to the kitchen . . . as—as I said earlier,' she stammered defensively, and bent to retrieve the other two forms from the floor, where they had slipped from her fingers when Thane first kissed her.

Edging up against the pillow, Thane linked his hands behind his head casually and flexed an indifferent shoulder. The movement set taut muscles rippling beneath the darkly tanned skin, making her aware of the unquestioned strength that could so effortlessly have overpowered her if he had felt so inclined.

'Then I guess you'd better deliver them, hadn't you?' he drawled in the same satirical fashion as before.

Adair gazed at him doubtfully, strangely feeling as if something else needed to be said, but not knowing quite what. Then, sighing, she gave a sombre nod and, without looking in his direction again, let herself out of the unit quietly.

So she had believed he couldn't ravish her in a motel full of people! Adair recalled her earlier reassuring contention with a despairing groan. God, he had all but seduced her—and *she* had offered about as much objection as a soggy sponge!

'So just what do you think you were doing last night, sneaking back into Thane's room after everyone had left?' demanded Rachel on a furious, grating note the minute she saw Adair the following morning as the younger girl was beginning her cleaning round of the units. 'And don't bother to deny it!' she continued immediately with a snarl. 'I *saw* you creep back in there, and *not* leave again until long *after* midnight!'

She had been watching! Why? Because she too had intended returning to Unit Five? Whatever the reason, Adair still couldn't control the flush that stained her cheeks at the memories evoked even as she did her best to appear unruffled.

'Not that it's any concern of yours,' she began quietly, pointedly, and gave an impassive shrug, 'but I returned to collect the breakfast menus I happened to have forgotten when I left.'

'How very convenient!' Rachel promptly sneered. 'And that took you the best part of an hour!'

'They'd become separated and it took a while to find them all,' Adair relayed with another nonchalant hunching of her shoulders.

'Were you even looking?'

The colour in Adair's cheeks deepened ungovernably and, seeing it, the blonde-headed girl burst into wrathful speech once more.

'No, I didn't think so!' she spat, her green eyes glittering. 'But if you know what's good for you, you'd better give Thane Callahan a wide berth in future, I can tell you!' She drew a harsh breath, her expression threatening. 'I'm not having some cheap little slut like you interfering in *my* plans!'

Adair gasped, her own temper starting to rise, although in her case it surfaced in an entirely different fashion. 'You mean you consider inconsequential, plain and dowdy little me ... competition?' she mocked in tones of exaggerated disbelief. 'Goodness, Rachel, how insecure you must be!' Pausing momentarily, she wasn't averse to allowing a pitying smile to shape her lips. 'And particularly where Thane's concerned, apparently.'

'I am nothing of the kind!' the other girl denied immediately, if a trifle shrilly. Then, as if suddenly remembering that in the courtyard there was every possibility of being overheard, she lowered her voice as she went on to scorn, 'As you'll find out, if you're stupid enough to believe Thane's ever likely to consider you anything but a handy convenience during his stay here in Ashvale! So why don't you just do yourself a favour and direct your attentions elsewhere?' It was she who smiled, patronisingly now.

'Oh, I was intending to,' Adair had no compunction in revealing truthfully. 'So you see there was no need for you to panic, after all.' With which goading remark she began pushing her trolley forward once more, and only then adding in much the same vein over her shoulder, 'Nevertheless, since I have never actively encouraged him, you may find it would aid your—er—plans considerably, of course, if you could somehow persuade him to give *me* a miss too! I would certainly appreciate it if you could, I can assure you.'

From behind her came the splutterings of pent-up fury and outrage, although only until the sound of a door closing brought them to an abrupt halt, whereupon she heard Rachel call out in lilting tones, 'Thane! I was just coming to see you. I thought I might accompany you and Egan when you visit the Quinns. That is, if you have no objection, of course.' The last was added on a simperingly sweet note that had Adair executing a disgusted grimace as she hurriedly let herself into the nearest vacant unit.

For her part she wanted no contact with either of them, although the thought of Thane perhaps following her into the room, as he had once before, did cause her some moments of trepidation as she waited half expectantly, half apprehensively for some sign of his approaching presence. When no such signal eventuated, she chanced a quick peep through the window, but only to find the courtyard devoid of people altogether.

Which, of course, was the best result she could have hoped for, she decided as she set about stripping the sheets from the beds in the unit. After all, hadn't that been her own decision only that morning? To keep out of Thane's sight, and thereby ensure a significant distance was maintained between them, as often as it was possible to do so. If she had needed any confirmation of her own contention, surely Rachel's claim that Thane merely saw her as a handy convenience—no matter even if imparted purely out of spite—had proved that beyond doubt!

So, with her resolve firmly in place, Adair made certain she remained busy *and* inconspicuous for the rest of the day, as well as the couple following. Although, as it happened, she had to admit that Thane showed no desire to speak to her either. A circumstance that, to her mind, merely helped prove that, having failed to get her into bed with him, he had no interest in her any more.

And that being so, she supposed she could claim to have won their battle of wills, and as a result found it difficult to understand why she seemed to have to keep *telling* herself she was pleased and relieved with the outcome, and not spontaneously experiencing those emotions as she would have expected.

Instead, her only impromptu thoughts appeared to centre exasperatingly around Thane, and the more so when she noticed that whenever he and his father left the motel, not only Rachel usually accompanied them, but her own sister, and as often as not, young Dimity too! And what an extremely gratifying experience that must be for him, with *three* doting females all vying for his attention! Adair scorned acidly.

However, her scorn was soon to be replaced with entirely different, and decidedly more worrying, emotions once her sister caught up with her just after lunch on the day prior to the Callahans' departure.

'I wanted to have a word with you in private,' Narelle disclosed quietly—self-consciously?—as they were leaving the dining-room. 'Do you have time to come to my room?'

'Of course,' Adair agreed readily, but wondering just what was coming, all the same.

Once inside her sister's room, Adair sank down on to the end of the bed, but Narelle remained standing, her whole stance portraying an uncustomary awkwardness that immediately had the younger girl eyeing her with a frown.

'Well?' she prompted watchfully.

Narelle flushed, and averted her gaze. 'Egan's invited me—and Dimity, of course—to spend the rest of the school holidays at Castlereagh,' she disclosed in a rush, and only then glancing at her sister from the corner of her eye to gauge her reaction.

Astonishment was the first emotion to register, which was responsible for the dubiously quizzed, 'Castlereagh?'

'His and Thane's property at Nannawarra.'

The mention of the younger man had Adair suddenly noticing the extra sparkle in her sister's hazel eyes, the becoming glow in her cheeks, and she gave a despairing shake of her head. 'Oh, Narelle, you're not still harbouring hopes of Thane, are you? I know you've been seeing a lot of him these last few days, but ...'

'No, not Thane,' the older girl cut in with a disclaiming wave of her hand. She paused, her colour rising noticeably. 'Egan.'

*'Egan!'* Adair echoed, looking as stunned as she sounded. 'But he's married, isn't he?'

'He was, but his wife died shortly after Thane was born.'

'And you're now saying...' Adair came to a halt, shaking her head in disbelief, and unable to actually put her incredible thoughts into words.

Now that she had actually committed herself, Narelle appeared to have no such difficulty, however. 'That I like him, that he likes me, and that I'd be pleased if something permanent developed from our relationship? Yes!' she nodded decisively.

'But he's much too old for you!' Adair blurted unthinkingly.

'No, he's not!' Narelle defended so sharply that it made her sister realise just how seriously she viewed the matter. 'There's only eighteen years' difference in our ages, and it's not as if those years have treated him harshly either. He's still a lot fitter than a number of younger men I could name.'

It was all becoming too much for Adair. 'But— but I thought—or at least suspected on occasion— that you were only in his company so much because it was a convenient way to—er—be where Thane was.'

'Yes—well, I must admit that did have something to do with it initially,' Narelle confessed somewhat guiltily. 'But the more I got to know him, the more my feelings towards him started to change. He's a very considerate and understanding man, and he treats me with respect, *not* as if I'm only interested in one thing just because I have an illegitimate child!' She paused, and a pleasurable smile caught at the corners of her mouth. 'He's also very good with Dimity. Once again, not like others who have only seen her as an unwanted encumbrance.' Her smile took an oblique turn. 'And precisely as you've pointed out on a number of occasions, I might add.'

Adair nodded, if a trifle bemusedly. 'And—and speaking of Dimity...what does she think of him?'

'Oh, she likes him very much!'

'As well as the idea of visiting his property?'

'More so,' Narelle replied with a laugh. 'Particularly in view of the fact that both Egan and Thane have promised to help her improve her polocrosse game.'

Yes, that would appeal to Dimity all right, Adair mused drily, then fell to chewing at her lip in frowning meditation. 'And does she also know what you're—hoping will eventuate from this visit?' A sudden thought flashed into her mind. 'For that matter, is—Egan of the same mind too?'

Narelle lifted a diffident shoulder, her expression becoming tinged with self-consciousness once more. 'I—well, nothing's been put into so many words as yet...it's still a little early for that.' She inhaled deeply. 'But I gained the impression that that was why he made the offer.'

A feasible assumption, Adair supposed.

'While as for Dimity...' her sister continued, 'well, no, I haven't actually discussed it with her in those terms. I thought it best to wait and see how matters progress first...and to see whether she even likes the life out west, of course. I wouldn't want to make a decision that would cause her any unhappiness.'

'You seem to have it all worked out,' Adair commented with a half-smile. If it was truly what her sister wanted, then she would be the first to wish her well. Narelle deserved better from life than she had received to date. 'And that being the case, I guess there's not much else I can say but to hope you have an enjoyable time and that everything proceeds as you would like it to.' She began rising to her feet.

'Except there is one small thing,' put in Narelle quickly. She hesitated. 'I'd like you to come with us.'

'*M-me!*' Adair just managed to get out, aghast, as an unreasoning sense of panic abruptly seemed to grip her and she descended heavily on to the bed again. Lord, she didn't want to spend a week and a half out there! Not in such close proximity to Thane Callahan, at any rate! the even more disrupting thought immediately followed. She struggled for composure. 'Whatever for? You're surely not suggesting you need a chaperon, of all things, in this day and age!' with a forced little laugh.

'Well, since I did want to ensure there could be no such possible misconstructions...'

'Then doubtless Dimity will be quite sufficient!' Adair was quick to propose.

'Although hardly in the same way another adult would be!' her sister was equally fast to counter. Her gaze sought Adair's hesitantly. 'Besides, it's such a big step to contemplate when you also have a child to consider that—that I think I might like a second opinion, or even just some moral support from someone I know and trust, if it comes to that.'

Being appealed to in such an anxious manner made Adair squirm inwardly for not immediately agreeing to the request. But she did have her own peace of mind to take into account, after all, and as a result she temporised, 'Mum could do that as well as, if not better, than I could.'

'Except that, on such short notice, she would never countenance leaving the cooking here in someone else's hands entirely, *and*...' Narelle fixed her with a ruefully wry glance ' ... you know as well as I do that, deep down, Mum is still so embarrassed at having an unmarried daughter with a child around that she'd automatically be in favour of any move, no matter what, if only it resulted in my marriage.'

A more than likely possibility, Adair had to concede, sighing, and she cast about frantically for another evasion. 'But with you away there'll be so much more work to be done here, and—and you're forgetting, *I* haven't even been invited to visit their property,' she submitted not a little triumphantly.

'Yes, you have,' Narelle contradicted with obvious pleasure, but conversely sending her sister's shoulders slumping. She gave an almost shy smile. 'As a matter of fact, I did sort of mention something of the sort to Egan, and he was quite agreeable that you accompany us. So you see you've no worries in that regard. As well, naturally I sounded out Mum before actually saying anything to you, and...'

'She fully supported the idea, I suppose,' deduced Adair, grimacing. It wasn't that their mother would willingly see either of her daughters unhappy, she knew, but once again, if there was the least likelihood of it helping to lead to the marriage of at least one of them, then she would be all for it. But at the same time it meant she herself was left with the same problem, and with all ready excuses exhausted, she was reduced to wailing helplessly, 'Narelle, I'm sorry, but I just don't want to go!'

'I wouldn't have guessed,' her sister surprised her by retorting in dry tones. 'But why? Because of Thane?'

Adair's breath caught in her throat. 'Why should he have anything to do with it?'

Narelle laughed. 'Oh, come on, love!' she exhorted. 'I doubt if it escaped anyone's notice that for almost the entire weekend you were wherever he was...or vice versa.' The amendment was hastily made as she saw the younger girl's indignant expression.

'So?' tautly.

'So maybe he did manage to get under your guard just a little, after all, eh?'

More than a little, if she did but know it! reflected Adair irritably. Not that she intended revealing as much, nevertheless. Quite the reverse, in fact. 'And do you really believe that's likely?' she pushed out with a scornful half-laugh. 'I mean, I was the one to warn *you* on Friday night not to have anything to do with him...and you may also have even noticed that we haven't been in each other's company *at all* since the weekend.'

'In that case, it would appear you have nothing to worry about, then, wouldn't it?'

Adair pressed her lips together. 'I wasn't aware I'd said it *was* Thane who worried me!'

'Well, something apparently does!' A trace of exasperation began edging into Narelle's voice.

'No, it doesn't,' Adair denied defensively. 'You know horses and the land, or—or anything like that, have never held any attraction for me. I'm just not interested in going bush, that's all.'

'Not even as a favour to me? Because it means so much to me?' queried Narelle part disappointedly, part pleadingly.

Adair couldn't hold her gaze. She supposed she was being lousy when it obviously did mean so much to her sister. And all because of one man! the taunting thought surfaced. It was enough to have her squaring her shoulders determinedly and assenting, 'All right, all right, if it means so much to you, I'll come!'

'Oh, thank you! I'm so glad!' With her face wreathed in a relieved smile, Narelle hugged her fondly. 'And you won't be sorry, I'm sure!'

Keeping her actual thoughts on that score to herself, Adair merely half smiled encouragingly and acceded, 'No, maybe I won't.' She simply hoped she could say much the same, and mean it, when she returned.

## CHAPTER SEVEN

AFTER picking up a co-member of Thane's polocrosse team who had also remained in town—a young man of about twenty-three by the name of Miles Pearson—they left for Nannawarra in two vehicles shortly after breakfast the following morning. Even so, it was still approaching the middle of the afternoon before they arrived at the small and neat, but widely laid out town. The great width of the main street, the same as in so many other bush towns, had been determined in days gone past by the need for long teams of yoked bullocks to be able to turn in it.

Here Miles left them—or rather, Thane and Rachel, with whom he had been travelling—while the rest of them continued on for another half an hour or so until reaching the Callahans' property, Castlereagh. When the homestead and surrounding outbuildings finally came into view, and Dimity alighted in order to open and then close again the last gate, Adair expelled a thankful breath.

It had been a long journey. It was the first time for all three members of her family to have travelled so far west—to what Adair supposed could legitimately be called the outback—but whereas she had merely viewed the scenery absently and in silence as it changed from rolling hills to broken sandstone ridges, and then vast open grasslands that

stretched to the horizon in every direction, Dimity
had exclaimed exuberantly at everything new she
saw, asked innumerable questions and chattered
incessantly, and by doing so made the trip appear
even longer at times.

'Gee, your house is big!' she now remarked in
admiring tones to Egan on resuming her seat in the
vehicle as they continued on to the veranda-enclosed
homestead that seemed to sprawl haphazardly in
all directions, and as a result should have looked
an architectural disaster, but with its attractive
shading trees and climbing vines somehow managed
to appear pleasantly mellow and invitingly
comfortable instead. 'Much bigger than I thought
it would be,' she added truthfully.

'Yes—well...' Egan turned to smile at her.
'There've been large numbers in the Callahan family
on occasion over the years, so those generations
that required extra space just added bits here and
there,' he explained. 'Also, the connecting
breezeways—much appreciated in the summer—
tend to add to its appearance of size too.'

Dimity nodded, leaving it to her mother to
hazard, 'It gets very hot in summer?'

Egan cast her an almost apologetic glance.
'Usually around forty degrees.' He hesitated. 'And
sometimes, if there's a hot westerly blowing from
the centre, it can even start pushing fifty.'

While her sister made some laughing quip in
reply, bringing a relieved look to Egan's features,
Adair pulled a graphic face and could only be
grateful that she had arrived in winter. Although
once she alighted from the station wagon outside
the homestead, she immediately began to realise just

how different was the climate from that on the
coast. It hadn't been so noticeable while in the vehicle, but now she was aware of a decidedly cold
wind that had her shivering involuntarily, and she
was reminded that it was quite common in the
outback for the overnight temperature to drop
below freezing during the winter months.

Seeing her shiver, Egan Callahan promptly began
ushering them inside. There were a couple of steps
leading to the insect-screened veranda, and then
they entered a wide central, gleaming timber-lined
hallway that gave on to a number of rooms.

Shown into the first, Adair surveyed the spacious
room with its similarly timber-lined walls and
sheepskin-dotted floors consideringly, deducing that
this was part of the original building. Large enough
to accommodate a couple of damask-covered sofas
and four matching armchairs, complete with
padded footstools, the room also contained a
number of curved-legged tables, two of them
bearing suitably placed reading lamps, the other
adorned with bowls of beautifully arranged dried
flowers. There was also an old roll-top desk with
an accompanying high-backed chair located between two sets of french doors; and a couple of
bookshelves, containing more framed family
photographs than books, on either side of a grated
fireplace that, although log-filled, still gave the appearance of rarely being used.

As, indeed, Adair suspected applied to the whole
room. It really was a sitting-room rather than a
living-room, she decided wryly, and she just
couldn't imagine either Egan Callahan or his ex-
ceedingly virile son contentedly relaxing after a hard

day on the property in such sedately arranged surroundings. And nor could her sister, she deduced,
when their glances chanced to meet.

In consequence, when Egan suggested they take
a seat, and he prepared to light the fire for them,
they both spoke up quickly, requesting him not to
go to any trouble on their account. 'I'm sure you
must have another room where you—er—normally
keep a fire alight,' concluded Narelle in whimsical
accents.

His lips twitched in acknowledgement. 'Well, it
being an all-male household, I must admit we don't
usually move far from the living or family rooms,'
he owned. 'However, with three young females as
guests, I did think we ought to at least make an
effort to...'

'We would rather you didn't,' Narelle cut in to
advise. 'Otherwise we'll just feel we're causing extra
work for you.'

'And unless, of course, you don't consider us
good enough to be invited into your living and
family rooms,' Adair ventured to insert jokingly.

Egan laughed, looking pleased by their decision.
'All right, then...'

'What on earth are you doing in here?' It was
Thane's voice that suddenly intervened now as he
appeared in the doorway with Rachel beside him.
She had accompanied them to the property because, as a near neighbour, her brother would
collect her later. Then, lowering to the floor the
two cases he had been carrying, Thane rested his
hands on lean hips, a vaguely sardonic sweep
catching at the edges of his mouth as his eyes
scanned Adair particularly before returning to his

father. 'Or does this provide more scope for seclusion than the living-room?'

The comment had the older man's brows lifting slightly in surprise, but Adair's lowered wrathfully. If he thought he was going to placate his punctured ego at her expense, he could damn well think again!

'Actually, we'd only just finished asking your father *not* to make any special arrangements on our behalf,' she was pleased to be able to reply with a sweetly gibing smile. 'So why don't you just lead the way to this living-room?'

Momentarily, he didn't move, but merely stood looking down at her with a narrowed, measuring gaze that had her deliberately taunting smile faltering, and tiny prickles of trepidation abruptly tingling down her spine. Then he inclined his head lazily, and definitely more provoking than deferential.

'OK, if that's what you want, then so be it,' he drawled carelessly as he bent to retrieve the cases.

Adair watched him uneasily, unsure if there had been a message in his words or whether she had simply imagined it. The only thing she was positive about was that she should never have answered his initial remark at all! Since Saturday night she had been free of Thane's attention, but goading comments from her could possibly see that state of affairs ending. And that wasn't what she wanted at all . . . was it?

Meanwhile, Rachel seemed anything but satisfied with the arrangement. 'Oh, but I much prefer *this* room!' she put in on a querulous note. 'It's always been a favourite of mine . . . as you know!' A reproachful gaze was turned on Thane. '*And*

we've always used it when I've stayed here
previously!'

'Mmm, but I'm sorry, this time it appears you've
been outvoted,' he returned with such an indifferent shrug, despite the implied apology, that
Adair's eyes rounded in surprise. Perhaps not all
Rachel's wishes were always of paramount import-
ance to him, after all.

'Oh, but...' that girl immediately began to
protest. However, discovering Thane already to be
starting down the hallway with an easy long-legged
stride, she pursed her lips in annoyance, but had
no choice except to follow him, along with the
others.

When they reached it, the living-room, as Adair
had imagined, proved to have a much more relaxed
atmosphere, and was far more masculine in appearance, not surprisingly. Here, the furniture was
of a more solid construction; from the obviously
well-used hide-covered armchairs beside the large
fireplace to the deep brown leather-upholstered
chesterfields, and even the sturdy low tables, that
she suspected had had many a booted foot rested
on them over the years. Here too were the books
that had been missing from the sitting-room,
stacked on shelves that covered an entire wall, as
well as an expensive-looking stereo system.

Through connecting double doors, the family
room appeared just as casually arranged, but evidently set aside for different pursuits, containing
as it did an assortment of easy chairs, a television,
a heavy green-baized snooker table, a dartboard,
and a small inlaid table already set with chess pieces,

the walls being decorated with a multitude of polocrosse trophies and ribbons.

No sooner had Egan seen Narelle and Adair seated—Dimity making herself comfortable on a chesterfield with a book on horses she had immediately located—than he set about lighting a warming fire. On the other hand, Rachel, obviously at home in the place, and declining a chair, made for one of the doorways at the far end of the room.

'I'll make some tea, and see about beginning preparations for dinner,' she advised airily.

Not wanting anyone to think she expected to be waited on, Adair made to rise from her seat. 'I'll give you a hand,' she offered, despite her reluctance to spend any time in the other girl's company.

Looking up, his glance just a trifle—impatient?—as it came to rest on Rachel, Egan immediately vetoed, 'No, it'll be right. Neither of you need bother. I'll be finished here in a couple of minutes, then I'll be able to make the tea. While as for dinner, Thane and I . . .'

'I know, I know! The pair of you have always managed very well on your own in the past,' Rachel broke in to coo soothingly as if talking to a child. 'But you must admit it's a nice change for you when I take over while I'm here, and I *do* introduce you to lots of new dishes, don't I?'

Most of which Egan, at least, would rather have forgone if his expression was any indication, surmised Adair wryly.

'So you just leave it all to me, and I'll have something special whipped up in no time,' Rachel continued brightly, evidently determined to have her own way in this at least. Her green eyes swung to encompass Adair. 'I don't need any help, either. You can do the cleaning up afterwards.' With which haughty direction she turned for the door once again. 'Oh, you might send Thane to me in the kitchen, though, once he's finished bringing in the luggage. Just in case I've forgotten where something's kept,' she suggested with a trill of laughter before disappearing.

Egan immediately exhaled heavily. 'Here goes a week's supplies,' he forecast in an ironic growl. 'She always cooks as if it's a party for twenty, and in spite of all that it's still not even as if it's a decent feed when she's finished!'

Then why did he let her do it? Out of deference to his son? mused Adair. A tempting thought occurred. But his son was absent temporarily, and as Egan obviously wasn't altogether in favour of the situation...

'Why don't you go and supervise, then?' she suggested helpfully, although not altogether only on his account. She wasn't averse to a little retaliation for Rachel's derogatory rebuff of herself either. 'I can finish laying and lighting the fire for you,' She suspected it could also have been consideration for their comfort that hindered him.

'Hmm...' Egan received her proposition with a whimsical twitching of his lips, and rose to his feet. 'Thank you, I may just accept that offer... if you have no objection either?' He sought Narelle's affirmation.

'I'll do better than that, I'll come with you,' she proposed with a smile, gaining her own feet.

Her company accepted with alacrity, the two of them left the room together, leaving Adair to approach the fire somewhat wryly. Not that she had the first idea of how to go about laying a fire, of course, but at the same time she supposed it couldn't be too difficult. Especially in view of the fact that there was no shortage of sawn logs in the box beside the fireplace, which she proceeded to pile on top of the paper Egan had already placed in the grate.

In spite of all her efforts, however, and after a considerable number of attempts, she was no closer to actually getting the logs to light than when she started. And to her disgust, she seemed to be getting progressively more ash-stained each time she pulled the wood out in order to add more paper. *That* was only too willing to burn very rapidly! she noted with a direful grimace as yet another of her efforts came to nought. Nor was her patience or composure helped at all by Dimity's innocent comment that it was getting colder, or by Thane's ensuing entry into the room.

Taking in the scene, and her appearance, his brows promptly rose ironically. 'Thought the chimney could do with a bit of a clean, did you?' he drawled with infuriating humour.

The sound of her niece's smothered giggle had Adair's equanimity deteriorating even further. 'No, I'm just trying to light this damned stupid fire!' she flared.

'With all the ability of previous experience?' mockingly.

'I don't *have* any previous experience! I've never needed it in the climates where I've lived!' she retorted, not a little disdainfully. 'Although heaven only knows why it won't catch, anyway!' Her expression became somewhat accusing. 'The wood must be damp, or—or something!'

Thane's lips sloped provokingly. 'How about . . . simply the wrong kind?'

*The wrong kind!* 'Then why put it here?'

'Because it's the right kind *once* the fire's going, and since it's rarely not alight in winter when we're home, we keep the kindling outside,' he explained, but whether indulgently or patronisingly Adair couldn't quite decide. 'If you like, I'll get some for you, and . . .' a chafing grin came into play, 'you can have a wash in the meantime. There's a bathroom on the other side of the hall.' Turning on his heel, he headed for the door that led on to the veranda.

Adair wrinkled her nose at his broad back, but gratefully made use of the bathroom all the same, and was back beside the fireplace once more when he returned with a bundle of much smaller wood.

'So how come you were attempting to make and light the fire in the first place?' Thane eyed her speculatively as he sank lithely on to his haunches next to her.

Pretending to be engrossed in placing more paper in the grate, Adair kept her gaze averted. 'Because I offered,' she replied as offhandedly as possible.

'Despite not having a clue as to what to do?'

'I didn't realise it was likely to prove such a problem, but something else required your father's attention.' She carefully refrained from revealing just what, guessing he wouldn't approve.

Thane merely nodded, and she was relieved when he applied his attention to adding the kindling to the paper and setting it alight, and thereby forestalling any further questions. In no time at all, the flames began licking at the wood, bringing it quickly to blazing, and thankfully warming life.

'Now...you add the logs,' advised Thane so drily that involuntary colour stained Adair's cheeks as she watched him proceed to build the fire higher.

'I'd already guessed that,' she retorted exasperatedly in sarcastic accents, her only consolation being that, with the fire now burning strongly, his departure doubtless wouldn't be long coming. An event she was also only too willing to hasten when a sound from the direction of the kitchen prompted her memory.

'Oh, by the way, Rachel requested...no, instructed,' she amended, deliberately precise, and not a little pleasurably, 'that you be sent to her in the kitchen once you finished bringing in the luggage. I'm sorry for forgetting to mention it earlier, although I'm sure she'll forgive you once she realises it wasn't your fault.' She dared to cast him a provoking smile.

Still squatting beside her in front of the fire, Thane crooked a challenging brow and inclined his dark head closer. 'And just what makes you think I either need, or want, her forgiveness?' he enquired in a smooth, low murmur, preventing Dimity from hearing.

He was so close that Adair could feel his breath against her warming cheek, making her feel suddenly breathless. 'I—well, you have spent just about *all* your time in her company these last few days,' she pushed out shakily, but with dismayingly little of the mockery she wanted to express.

'That can easily be rectified.' His long-lashed, slate-grey eyes locked disturbingly with hers.

His meaning was plain and she swallowed convulsively. Then a consuming anger engulfed her and she broke the unsettling contact with a violent shake of her head. 'Oh, yes, that's it, off with one and on with another!' she gritted. 'It makes no difference to you, does it? After all, one's as convenient as the next!'

'Although not to any great extent, in your case, I would have said!' Thane promptly mocked on a derisive note.

'No, thank God!' Adair was perfectly amenable to endorsing, her voice starting to rise as she scrambled to her feet. 'I'm glad to say I learnt my lesson well where treacherous men are concerned! I can also assure you that I'm more than content with my presently male-less life, so if it's variety you're looking for...' She came to a sudden gulping, embarrassed halt on noticing that not only had Dimity begun to take an interest in the conversation, but that the door to the kitchen had opened as well and that Narelle, with Egan and Rachel not far behind, was bringing in a tray of tea.

'Oh, don't stop on our account.' Rachel was the first to speak, maliciously. 'We've heard all you've had to say thus far.'

Adair's face flamed, although her sister's ensuing shake of the head in denial did allow her to breathe a little easier, the more so when Egan added his own kindly assurance, 'Well, not strictly speaking, at any rate.' A curious look in his son's

direction and he went on in what Adair suspected
was a deliberately alleviating, genial fashion, 'But
don't you take any nonsense from him, Adair. He
can be an aggravating devil at times...as I know
only too well.'

Adair half smiled weakly. 'Oh, I think I'll be able
to manage,' she asserted, if more to convince herself
than anyone else.

'Not that I can see why it's apparently automatically assumed Thane was the cause of their argument!' put in Rachel sharply, giving him the
benefit of a sweetly supportive smile as she accepted a cup of tea from Narelle and seated herself
beside the fire.

'Mmm...' Thane himself seemed to give that
point some consideration before musing in sardonically drawled tones, 'Although what I would
really like to know is...and just who will be keeping
Adair in line?'

Somewhat recovered now, and staunchly with-
holding the sniping, 'Not you, if that's what you're
thinking!' that initially came to mind, Adair kept
her features carefully schooled. Even when he
perched himself casually, unexpectedly, on the arm
of the chesterfield where she had taken a seat.

'I'm not in the habit of stepping—out of line,'
she returned with all the primness she could muster.

'But I am?' He raised a sardonic brow.

Adair swallowed, wondering if he was attempting to bait her into continuing their last
dispute, or saying something about Saturday night.
Just in case, she deliberately steered the conversation in another direction. 'Apparently...

according to your father.' She allowed herself the barest of mocking half-smiles.

Egan laughed, but Thane's lips merely shaped obliquely. 'Then I guess I'll just have to be on my best behaviour, won't I?'

Unable to ignore the temptation, Adair slanted him a graphic look from beneath the veil of her curling lashes. 'You mean, you're admitting there *is* room for improvement?' she purred.

He smiled lazily, his grey eyes lingering on her curving lips so measuringly that she involuntarily ran the tip of her tongue across their suddenly dry surface. 'I'll leave that for you to judge,' he proposed in an almost too smooth voice under cover of his father's laughing response to her riposte, and Rachel's denigration of it, before rising to his feet with unconscious grace and making for the couch facing the fire where he subsided on to the deep cushions, stretching out comfortably—and propped his feet on the edge of the table.

Taken aback by the feeling of loss that abruptly assailed her at his departure, Adair did her best to keep her attention fixed on Egan's and Narelle's ensuing conversation in an effort to dispel the alarming emotion, and after a time she was successful. But she assiduously refrained from glancing in Thane's direction, all the same.

In fact, it wasn't until some time later, while she was getting ready for dinner, that she even spoke to him again. Although, once again, she would have preferred it otherwise, for on leaving the bathroom after showering, she found herself suffering more than a moment's discomposure on suddenly being confronted by his bare-chested figure leaning negligently against the wall outside, with only a towel tied loosely about his lean hips.

She supposed it came naturally to him, owing to there normally being only the two men in the house, but coming from such a female-dominated atmosphere as she did, and even though she told herself she saw the same every time she went to the beach, she still couldn't prevent a surge of self-conscious heat from warming her face. Just as it had the previous Saturday when she had first confronted him similarly clad. Or perhaps it was simply the thought of what had followed on that occasion that was making her feel so unnerved now, the unbidden thought followed, and had her flushing even more discomfitedly as a result.

'I—I'm sorry if I've kept you waiting,' she pushed out unsteadily.

Thane flexed a muscular shoulder, a slow smile twitching at the corners of his mouth as he eased himself upright. And for all the world as if he knew precisely the effect he was having on her! she decided with a spurt of fortifying anger. 'No worries, I haven't been here long.'

'You couldn't have used the other bathroom?' ironically. She knew there were two of them.

'Uh-uh! Rachel's in there, and knowing the care—and time,' drily voiced, 'she takes to ensure she looks her best...'

'Unlike me, you mean?'

Thane surveyed her slowly, unsettlingly, from head to toe. 'Well, you do have a preference for the shapeless and unflattering, don't you, angel?' he drawled.

Adair inhaled sharply. So he was back to criti-
cising the way she dressed, was he? In retaliation,
she permitted her own eyes to glide the length of
his intensely masculine form too. 'Although I do
at least *wear* some clothes!' she retorted pointedly
and, lifting her chin in dismissal, set off down the
hall.

Thane laughed. A warm, vibrant sound that
loosed ungovernable butterflies in her stomach.
'You look better without!' he called after her provokingly, and Adair felt her face crimson with
mortification.

Nevertheless, by the time she reached her
bedroom, she had come to a decision. All right,
tonight she would wear something different! As it
happened, she had, in a moment's weakness,
brought some of her more becoming outfits with
her. Although solely in order to put Rachel out of
countenance, of course! she reminded herself
hastily as she set about sorting through her case for
something suitable.

As a result, when she entered the living-room
again shortly before dinner, it was with something
of a challenging air. Clad in chocolate brown snug-
fitting pants and a lime-green stretch-knit top that
faithfully outlined every curve, she was well aware
of just how different she looked. The more so since,
in a heady rush of defiance, she had even applied
a little make-up. A touch of becoming eyeshadow
and mascara, and a trace of glossy lipstick only,
but when emphasising already striking features
against her naturally creamy complexion, the effect
was quite dramatic. Her hair she had brushed until

it shone with sparks of fire, and left it swirling about her shoulders in a mass of waves and curls.

'Oh, Aunty Adair, you do look pretty!' exclaimed Dimity spontaneously on sighting her, making her relative flush as the remark immediately made her the centre of attention.

'That's an understatement!' smiled Egan gallantly as he detached himself from Narelle and strode towards her. Of Thane or Rachel there was no sign, and Adair wasn't certain whether she was disappointed or thankful. 'Would you care for a drink? Dinner shouldn't be too long... although you can never tell when Rachel's at the helm,' he added wryly.

Adair nodded, still feeling somewhat self-conscious, but trying hard not to show it. 'Then perhaps a sherry, or—or something similar, thank you,' she murmured, accompanying him to the bar cabinet that stood in one corner. And in an effort to match his levity, 'You weren't able to—er—regain complete control of your kitchen, then?'

Having determined her preference from among the assortment available, Egan poured the wine into a glass and handed it to her. 'No, not entirely,' he conceded with a rueful half-laugh. 'Although we did manage to prevail upon Rachel sufficiently to restrict her efforts to a meal instead of a cocktail party. Oh, I could have put my foot down and ordered her from the kitchen altogether, I suppose, but...' he smiled and shrugged tolerantly, 'I guess she's only trying to do us a favour, after all, and I must admit it *is* pleasant to have some relief from preparing meals for a change.'

His last was a sentiment Adair could fully understand, but his assumption that Rachel was merely
doing them a favour she found difficult to believe.
And before she could stop herself, she was haz-
arding part sardonically, part flatly, 'You don't
think—Thane might be the reason for her endeav-
ours?' Such as, in order to impress him with her
culinary efficiency and ability she added silently
with a grimace.

Egan seemed to give the matter some thought,
somewhat to Adair's surprise that he should need
to. 'Well, that's always a possibility, I suppose,' he
allowed slowly at length. 'Rachel does like to cast
her eye in many a direction . . . and usually all at the
one time,' with a smile. He paused, his expression
sobering a little. 'However, while on the subject of
Thane . . .' He hesitated again, as if unsure of his
ground, then plunged on in an earnest vein, 'I don't
know what he said to upset you this afternoon, and
perhaps it's even best that I don't know, but I meant
what I said about you not letting him get under
your skin. I mean, I did notice over the weekend
that matters—er . . .' he cleared his throat '. . . didn't
always appear harmonious between you, but I
would very much like you to enjoy your stay here,
and unfortunately that's not likely to occur if he's
allowed to continue causing you distress.'

Adair swallowed. 'Oh, but he doesn't really!' she
immediately tried to reassure him, and took a
steadying mouthful of sherry. Lord, if he said anything to Thane, there was no telling what the
outcome might be! 'We just fail to see eye-to-eye
on a number of things, that's all.' She did her best
to make light of it. 'Besides, as I also said this

afternoon, I can manage him.' In truth, it was
herself she failed to manage as often as not.

'Well, as long as you're sure...' He still didn't
look entirely convinced.

'Oh, yes!' She forced a confident smile on to her
lips, and was thankful when he nodded slowly and
went on to talk about something else as Narelle
joined them.

When Thane put in an appearance a short time
later, apologising for having been caught up on the
phone, at almost the same moment Rachel advised
from the doorway at the other end of the room that
dinner was ready, her expression registering surprise as her gaze came to rest on Adair momentarily before she turned on her heel with something
of a glower and stalked back into the kitchen.

But while the others finished their drinks and
began making for the dining-room, Thane remained where he was, his glance fixed on Adair.

'Well, well, and what brought this on?' he questioned, eyeing her clothes significantly. 'Or dare I
hope it's a result of our last conversation concerning the subject?'

Feeling the heat of embarrassment burn her
cheeks at the memory of that last conversation,
Adair took a long sip of her drink and hunched a
defensive shoulder. 'No, I—I just felt like a change,
that's all.'

'A permanent change?' watchfully.

Under the impact of his ebony-framed gaze,
Adair felt stifled by the heat that suddenly seemed
to envelop her, and she was unwillingly conscious
of how dangerously attractive he was. Flustered by
the feeling, she answered without thinking. 'And

what's it to you if it is or not?' she flared. 'Until this afternoon, you haven't been sufficiently interested to even speak to me since the weekend!' She promptly gave a chagrined gasp as she realised she had said more than she intended.

In response, Thane's mouth slanted crookedly. 'I thought that was how you preferred it.'

'I—well, of course I d-do,' she stammered, trying desperately to recover lost ground. Finishing her drink, she deposited the glass on the table somewhat unsteadily. 'I just meant that—it's still my decision to make.'

'Was I suggesting otherwise?' he countered drily.

'N-o...' Adair conceded slowly. 'But...'

'Hurry up, you two, Rachel's already starting to fume!' interposed Narelle from the doorway in a wry stage whisper.

'Coming!' Thane began urging Adair ahead of him. 'I guess we'll just have to continue this after dinner.'

'There's nothing to *be* continued!' Her voice rose fractionally.

'You think not?'

Adair refused to reply. She had already given her answer to that question. She simply hoped that by the time dinner was concluded he would have forgotten the matter. And particularly in view of the fact that during the meal there were certainly enough instances to distract his attention. At least away from her clothing, she soon discovered after being seated—some distance from Thane, she noted thankfully, even if doubtlessly due to Rachel's manoeuvring—at the oval-shaped, polished mahogany table in the large and ornate dining-room.

Not unexpectedly, Rachel had placed herself closest to Thane, and did her best to monopolise his attention throughout the daintily prepared and rather exotic meal. Not that she was always successful, much to Adair's growing dismay when it became apparent that Egan Callahan stopped to listen to any remarks his son happened to address to Adair herself—and promptly made his feelings known, meaningfully even if pleasantly, if he considered them in any way out of order. And what comments of Thane's to herself weren't ever of the mocking or baiting variety? she groaned.

That Thane evidently believed his father's intervention had been brought about by her doing was reflected in his increasingly grim and tight-lipped expression. A fact that had Adair on tenterhooks for the remainder of the meal, and reluctantly acknowledging that, for once, she was going to have to seek him out in order to at least try and explain—if only to ensure it caused no dissension between him and his father, as she suspected it might possibly do. She didn't want that on her conscience as well!

However, actually speaking to him alone proved harder to accomplish than had been the decision to do so, for immediately they left the table, Rachel—obviously considering she had done sufficient, or at least all she was interested in doing—prevailed upon him to join her in a game of darts. Then, once Narelle and Adair, with Dimity's and Egan's assistance, had cleared away the remains of the meal, tidied the kitchen, and set the dishwasher going, it was only to find neither Thane nor Rachel in sight when they repaired to the living-room afterwards.

Nor had they reappeared by the end of the evening, so that when Egan placed a protective guard around the still glowing fire and they prepared to seek their beds, Adair sighed and supposed she was just going to have to wait until the morning to seek Thane out. Obviously Rachel had succeeded in capturing his undivided attention for the latter part of the evening at least—and she could guess just how!

Notwithstanding her surmise, she did still linger for a few more minutes after the others had departed—just in case—but when she heard no sounds other than the sporadic crackling of the subsiding fire and her own slightly deepened breathing, she pulled an acid grimace for her own naïveté in expecting Thane to leave the other girl's gratifying presence that night, and made for the hallway leading to her room.

About to turn into it, she almost collided with Thane as he rapidly entered the room. So he had managed to tear himself away from Rachel's arms, after all, was her initial, involuntary thought.

Then she had other things on her mind, as he promptly rasped in a savage tone she had never heard him use before, 'Not so fast, Adair! I want a word with you!'

'Fast!' she was startled into repeating incredulously as she automatically retreated a little further into the room. 'Then perhaps you should have dragged yourself away from your girlfriend a little earlier, because I've been here *all* evening!' A gibing nuance made an appearance.

'And as I've told you before . . . Rachel is not my girlfriend!'

'No, I was forgetting. You don't have girlfriends...just handy conveniences!' Adair charged scornfully.

A muscle jerked at the side of his taut jaw. 'And you're changing the subject, you bloody trouble-making little...!'

'No!' she broke in on him urgently, and hurriedly re-channelling her thoughts. She reached out a tentative hand, then thought better of it and let it fall again. 'Look, I know what you're thinking, but you're wrong!'

'Oh, yes?' A dark brow peaked in sarcastic disbelief.

'Yes!' she repeated doggedly. 'You think I put your father up to intercepting your comments aimed at me, but I didn't! I swear I didn't!' Her earnest blue eyes clung anxiously to glacial grey.

'Then who are you suggesting did? Narelle...Dimity? Or how about Rachel, perhaps?'

Ignoring the caustic mockery that was almost tangible, Adair shook her head vehemently. 'No, it was your father's own idea!' Pausing, she chewed discomfitedly at her lip. 'After hearing us arguing this afternoon, he—he seemed to think I needed...protection, I guess,' she concluded awkwardly.

There was no trace of any lessening of Thane's cynical regard. 'And how would you know that...if you hadn't spoken to him about it?'

'Because *he* mentioned it to me, not the other way round!' She exhaled heavily. 'He said he wanted my stay here to be an enjoyable one, but that he didn't think that it was likely to be if you

kept—upsetting me.' Her eyes lifted to his entreat-
ingly once more. 'I tried to tell him that it didn't
really bother me, but...' she shrugged helplessly,
'he apparently didn't believe me.'

When he didn't immediately speak, she turned
away in a defeated movement. 'Oh, hell, I knew I
should never have let Narelle talk me into accompanying her!' she despaired. 'I don't want your
father at odds with you because of me!' And,
glancing back at him over her shoulder with an
almost defiant look, 'Nor do I need anyone in-
terceding on my behalf where you're concerned
either, I might add!'

Thane inclined his head imperceptibly. 'Then I
guess there's only one course left open to us, isn't
there?'

'And that is?'

He shrugged. 'To call a truce...' He halted, his
expression eased a little as his mouth shaped
crookedly. 'Temporarily, at least.'

Adair released the breath she had been unconsciously holding and nodded quickly. Even a tem-
porary respite from his arbitrary and goading
comments would be most welcome.

'So shall we seal it with a drink?' he suggested
cursorily, raising an enquiring brow and making for
the bar as if taking her agreement for granted. 'I
don't know about you, but I could use something
warming, in any case. It's damn cold outside.'
Shrugging out of the sheepskin jacket that it only
then registered with her that he was wearing, he
slung it casually over the back of a chair and began
pouring two brandies.

'You've been outside?' Adair's own brows arched in surprise.

'Uh-huh!' He nodded as he turned to hand her one of the drinks he had just poured, and headed with the other for the couch in front of the fire. 'But not with Rachel, if that's what you're thinking,' he looked up from where he was lounging indolently on the deeply padded cushions to advise in speaking tones. 'Merely to check on the horses David brought back after the carnival, and to have a word with our head stockman.'

From having been following him a trifle indecisively, Adair now angled her chin higher and swept towards one of the fireside chairs with a firmer tread. 'It matters little to me whether you were with her or not,' she snubbed.

'Although you were the first to bring her into the conversation by assuming I'd spent the evening with her,' Thane reminded her in an abrupt return to his usual lazily dry manner, and which left her unprepared for his sudden action in catching hold of her arm as she passed the couch, and pulling her down on to it beside him. 'It is supposed to be a truce...remember?' he drawled mock-reprovingly when she promptly made to protest.

'A suspension, yes...but not submission!' she tossed back on a gibing note, and purposely put a little more distance between them. 'Besides, why wouldn't I assume you'd been with her all evening? You disappeared together!'

'Even if not in the same direction,' whimsically.

'Oh!' At a loss to understand the feeling of satisfaction that spread through her, Adair took a sip of the bolstering spirit in her glass. 'I—well, I wasn't to know that.' Suddenly she frowned. 'Although if she wasn't with you, where has she been all evening?'

Thane shrugged an indifferent shoulder. 'Who knows? Rachel's a law unto herself. But since she was saying she was tired after the journey, it's more than probable she just went to bed, I guess.'

Without even saying goodnight—to Egan, at least? Or would that have been too much like advising everyone that she hadn't managed to keep Thane enthralled for as long as she wanted it to appear?

'And in that regard...' she abruptly realised Thane was continuing, 'how come you're the only one who hasn't apparently done the same, then?'

'Because I was hoping for a chance to explain about what happened at dinner.' She cast him an anxious sideways glance. 'And you do believe I didn't ask your father for his help, or—or complain to him about you, don't you, Thane?' As she recalled, he hadn't actually said so as yet.

'It's important to you that I do?' he countered, returning her gaze steadily.

Adair made a diffident movement with her head. 'It is the truth, and as I said earlier, I don't want to be the cause of you being in trouble with your father.'

'You don't think I deserve it?' His features turned lightly, banteringly, mocking.

'I—well, it does have a certain appeal, I must confess,' she dared to own in the same chaffing fashion. 'But even so...'

'His possible retaliation for my part in the matter worries you more than any revenge I might decide to exact on you for yours?' he interposed in ironic amusement.

Adair swallowed, took another mouthful of her drink, and tried hard to ignore the implication in his remark. 'Except that your father's involvement has nothing to do with me ... well, only indirectly,' she amended self-deprecatingly. 'Moreover...,' a dulcet half-smile suddenly made an appearance, 'you said yourself, we have a truce ... remember?'

Thane moved to deposit his glass on the table in front of them, his grey eyes taking on a sleepy look when he turned to face her again, and filling her with confusion as he unexpectedly raised a hand to smooth a finger over her softly parted lips. 'And if that's the reaction it brings, I obviously should have suggested it some time ago,' he murmured on a resonant note.

Flustered, Adair dragged her gaze from his and hurriedly disposed of her own glass. 'Yes—well, if you weren't so determined to cr██████████ all the time...' She strove to sou████████ least.

His hand moved to toy with a curl of her hair. 'Although I'm not being provoking now, am I?'

Perhaps not in the manner she had meant, but he was certainly provoking sensations she had no desire to experience! she realised in dismay, and she drew a ragged breath. 'No, you're simply avoiding giving a direct answer as to whether you believed what I had to say or not,' she just managed to push out, trying desperately to return the conversation to its original subject.

'Uh-uh!' Thane denied with a lazy smile that had the nerves of her stomach fluttering, his hand

moving to caress the nape of her neck now. 'I'm
merely allowing my actions to speak for me.' And
by inexorably increasing the pressure on her neck,
it was an easy matter for him to pull her down on
top of him as he lay lengthwise along the couch.
His arms stole round her, defeating her struggles
to rise.

'No, Thane!' Adair immediately half protested,
half pleaded, in something of a panic at his perturbing change of mood, and overpoweringly aware
of the hard muscular form pressed so disturbingly
against her from shoulder to knee. 'And—and
someone could come in here at any moment!' Her
voice rose apprehensively as she sought in vain to
push herself away from him.

He shook his head. 'They've all gone to bed,' he
asserted softly, and set his warm mouth to her
arching throat. 'Where we should be too.'

Adair was only too willing to nod her agreement.
_____ she qualified hastily, if a little
_____ g the need to display at least some
_____ wn. The heat from the fire, the intimacy
of her position, the sheer effort required to keep
her head away from his, all seemed to be com-
bining to induce a betraying sense of weakening resistance within her.

Thane merely set his lips to the wildly beating
hollow at the base of her throat, his tongue circling
it sensuously. 'Have I told you yet just how beautiful you look tonight?' he murmured against the
suddenly over-sensitive skin.

'N-no,' she stammered weakly, then could have
bitten her tongue out for having as good as implied
that he should do so.

'Well, you do.' The hand behind her head impelled her still closer so that his mouth could find the exposed underside of her jaw and she swallowed convulsively. 'So will you continue dressing the same way in future?'

'You want me to?' The words seemed to tumble out helplessly before she could put a halt to them.

His mouth tilted slightly with wry humour. 'You already know the answer to that.'

Adair flicked the tip of her tongue over her lips, then wished she hadn't when the action seemed to act like a target for Thane's darkened and disturbing gaze. 'I didn't bring many of these clothes with me,' she evaded on a breathless, uneven note.

'Even if they look only half as good, no one's going to complain, no matter how often you wear them,' he declared thickly, and finally brought her mouth into inescapable contact with his.

At the first compelling touch, Adair felt the last trace of resistance drain from her. There seemed little point in exerting such a straining pressure on her neck muscles now, she told herself. Not that that explained the reason for her instinctive response, but as Thane's lips moved so expertly, so stirringly against hers, willing them to part to the probing possession of his stroking tongue, she felt a burning warmth begin in her stomach and spread downwards, and all further thought was chased from her mind.

With one hand tangled within the chestnut cloud of her hair, immobilising her head, Thane ran the other along the length of her slender form, and she shook with the intensity of her own desires as she felt it slide beneath her top to begin caressing the smooth, bare skin of her back. Almost before she knew it, Adair's own fingers slipped upwards, first clinging to his shoulders and then curling tightly within his dark hair as her world rocked with emotions never previously experienced.

Momentarily, Thane relinquished her lips in order to rain light kisses over her cheeks, her eyes, and her slender throat, before reclaiming her eagerly waiting mouth with a searing hunger she responded to uninhibitedly. The strong fingers exploring the curving sweep of her back impatiently unclasped her hindering bra, and turned their attention to the rounded sides of her breasts as they thrust against the hard wall of his broad chest, stroking and massaging them sensuously so that the soft flesh began to swell and firm.

But when he started to ease her top upwards, to allow him greater access, it seemed to trigger an abrupt return of Adair's consciousness: the recollection of just how proficiently persuasive Thane had been in a similar situation once before, and a reluctant, alarming acknowledgement that she actually wanted him as much as he apparently wanted her!

'No!' she choked, breaking away from him swiftly and tugging her top back into place as she jumped to her feet. 'This—isn't what I stayed for.'

The dark fringes of Thane's lashes lowered slightly as he levered himself into a sitting position. 'I seem to have heard that before somewhere.'

Adair shifted uncomfortably and tried to slow her still racing breathing. 'Yes—well, I'm sorry, but nothing's changed,' she said stiffly in a futile attempt to convince herself as much as him.

'So it would appear.' A faint thread of mockery edged into his voice.

She hunched a deprecatory shoulder. 'Besides, it—it's not the kind of conduct usually expected of guests.'

'Oh, for God's sake ... !' Thane gave an exasperated, disbelieving shake of his head as he suddenly rose to his feet, making her take a couple of hasty steps backward. 'This is my bloody home!'

'Meaning, you always—carry on like this with female guests?'

'Is that what you think?'

Adair touched her teeth to her lower lip, her blue eyes lifting to his doubtfully. She didn't know quite what she believed at the moment. 'I don't really know you well enough to judge,' she said at length.

'Although you obviously don't believe in allowing that to stop you making *judgements*!' Thane retorted in roughened tones. 'God! That fiancé of yours really left you twisted in knots, didn't he?'

Although nowhere near the extent *he* was doing, Adair reflected miserably. She looped her hair back behind her ear with a shaky hand and ventured to gibe defensively, 'All because I refuse to keep your bed warm?'

'Because you can't even be honest enough with yourself, let alone anyone else, to even admit that you want to!' he growled.

Adair flushed. 'You don't know that!' she protested.

To her surprise, Thane smiled, a ruefully amused shaping of his attractive mouth that had her catching her breath. 'Go to bed, angel ... while I'm still inclined to allow you to cling to that mistaken belief!'

Briefly, she was tempted to offer further denials, if only as a face-saving exercise, but then he took a step towards her, and she rapidly decided to exchange pride for prudence, and fled.

Once inside her room, though, Adair leant back weakly against the door with her hands held to her burning cheeks. Oh...*hell*! she despaired. What was happening to her? Or what was *he* doing to her? she amended with a groan.

First he wanted her hairstyle changed, and she yielded. Then he wanted her clothes changed, and for one reason or another it seemed she had acquiesced there too. Now he wanted *her*, and, God help her, she wanted to comply with that as well! Didn't she have any will of her own any more? Or was it simply that subconsciously she found herself wanting to please—and attract, the addition came compulsively—Thane Callahan?

The reason behind such a possibility she shied away from nervously and, giving a rejecting shake of her head, she hurriedly made ready for bed.

## CHAPTER EIGHT

EARLY the next morning David Howell arrived to collect his sister. Rachel made it evident she was extremely loath to depart Castlereagh but, since neither Egan nor Thane saw fit to invite her to extend her visit, in the end she had no choice but to leave with her brother, albeit with ill-grace.

That David had also had female company with him—a pretty brunette, as it happened—only served to make Adair's expression a little less disgruntled than Rachel's as she watched the three of them drive away from the homestead. Was there a man who wasn't fickle? she wondered acrimoniously.

Standing next to her, Thane caught sight of her discontented features and lowered his head closer. 'So what's eating you this morning?' he drawled.

Her jaw lifted. 'I was just thinking about poor Stephanie! It didn't take David long to replace her, did it?' she retorted acidly.

'Although, as I recall, she was the one making most of the running,' he pointed out in dry tones.

A contention she couldn't altogether deny, Adair supposed, so didn't try to. She charged instead, 'With his active encouragement, of course!'

Thane shrugged. 'Why not?' He paused, and a faintly sardonic curve caught at the edges of his firm mouth. 'Or are even unattached males only ever supposed to restrict themselves to one female, in your prejudiced view?'

163

'Oh, no, that *would* be expecting too much,' she was quite amenable to agreeing, with equal mockery. 'After all, they would need to have at least some concept of what fidelity means, in order to practise it, wouldn't they? And we all know just how unlikely that is!' She sent him a gibing smile and turned to follow Narelle and Egan who, along with Dimity, were making their way across to the horse paddock.

'Uh-uh!' She was surprised when Thane's hand on her shoulder suddenly brought her to a halt before she could reach the veranda steps. 'They can do without you tagging along,' he stated peremptorily.

'Meaning?' Adair eyed him with not a little indignation.

'Meaning, they may prefer to be on their own,' he returned, irony predominant. 'Not to mention it no doubt helping them to come to any decision regarding their future.'

'Oh!' She bit her lip uncomfortably. So he was fully aware of the reason for her sister's visit. She had wondered. 'Then if I'm not allowed to accompany them, perhaps you'd care to inform me just how I am supposed to fill in my time while I'm here?' she enquired sarcastically.

'You can come with me.' His advice was goadingly delivered.

Not likely! 'Yes—well, if that's the choice, I think I'll stay in the homestead,' Adair promptly proposed with a saccharine smile.

'And thereby give the old man even more reason to believe you're not enjoying your stay?' He shook his head decisively. 'I think not, angel! You're just

going to have to make the best of it . . . the same as
I'm having to do!' His voice roughened fractionally. 'In any case, aren't you forgetting our
truce?' He smiled and tapped her irritatingly under
the chin.

Adair glared at him balefully. Supposed truce was
more like it, since it didn't appear to have lessened
his mocking and goading comments at all when his
father wasn't around! she smouldered. But as *she*
still didn't want to cause any dissension in the
household, and especially as their visit was so important to her own sister, it was becoming all too
patently obvious that she really had little option in
the matter.

'All right! So I tag along with you instead!' she
conceded finally on a heaved breath. And, squinting
past the outbuildings to the limitless sun-drenched
plains beyond, 'Am I permitted to ask, where to?'

'Since we're drenching today, the sheep yards, I
guess,' he relayed drily, already starting for the
steps. 'Oh, and you'd better wear this too.' He
pulled his wide-brimmed hat from his head and
settled it over her chestnut curls.

Automatically, Adair opened her mouth to
decline, then rapidly shut it again on stepping out
into the sunlight. The dazzling glare from the
ground was enough to contend with, she discovered, without suffering the sun's unimpeded rays
from above as well. 'Thank you,' she acknowledged his action in a subdued murmur. Her eyes
flicked dubiously upwards. 'But won't you need it?'

A lazy smile spread across Thane's features, his
white teeth gleaming against his darkly bronzed

skin. 'Not as much as you, if we're to protect that pretty face of yours.'

With her heart already hammering in traitorous response to his slow, easy smile, Adair now felt a self-conscious colour stain her cheeks, and she ducked her head quickly in an effort to prevent him realising just how disastrously he had affected her equilibrium. 'So it will take some time, then, this—this drenching?' she faltered at length when she had regained at least some control over her scattered defences.

Thane hunched a muscular shoulder off-handedly. 'Most of the day, more than likely.'

Adair nodded, relieved by the casualness of his answer even if not by the length of time she was apparently going to have to spend in his company, and would have continued on in silence if a niggling curiosity hadn't finally got the better of her.

'And—er—what do you think of my sister's and your father's relationship?' she quizzed tentatively.

'I've no objection to it, if that's what you mean,' Thane replied with a certain sardonic inflection that had her compressing her lips in vexed resentment. That hadn't been what she'd meant at all! 'In fact . . .' he continued in a more contemplative tone '. . . I'm inclined to think it could be what they both need. I suspect that, in their own ways, they're both somewhat lonely people.'

Adair frowned. 'But your father's had you for company, and—and Narelle's always had us.'

'Mmm, except that wasn't the type of loneliness I was meaning. Unlike some,' his expressive gaze left her in no doubt as to just who, 'there are people in this world who enjoy the company of the op-

posite sex, and *need* the fulfilment of a close male/
female relationship!'

To her amazement, Adair had begun to feel almost
at home by the time she had been at Castlereagh
for a week. No less astonishingly, she also found
herself experiencing an affinity for the life on a vast
property: the timelessness of her surroundings; the
crystal-clear air; the incredible sense of freedom,
of having room to move, provided by those broad
and shimmering horizons.

With Thane's guidance, she had participated in
numerous station activities, and even been per-
suaded to practise her own riding on occasion when
he had been demonstrating some of the finer points
of polocrosse for Dimity's eager benefit. Not that
she supposed she would ever attain the easy and
almost insolent familiarity with the saddle he displayed, or be able to swing into one with the lithe
grace he did, which never failed to stir a grudging
admiration within her.

There had also been a fascinating inspection of
the property by air in the Callahans' own plane; a
lazy day's fishing in one of the many earth dams
that provided the stock with water; and she had
even journeyed in to Nannawarra to watch the
club's teams at polocrosse practice, as well as attended another carnival. Only this occasion at a
town not nearly so far distant.

Through it all, she had also determinedly attempted to reject the wayward feelings that had
made their presence felt so perturbingly that first
night on the station, although to her dismay she

had discovered they weren't so accommodating as
to suffer dismissal quite so easily!

While as for Thane himself... He had been in-
formative, teasing, amusing, and sociable.
*But*...not once had he either tried to kiss her again,
or by so much as a look or action given her any
reason to suppose he thought of her any differently
from the way he did Dimity. In fact, she could only
have said he treated them both as if they were his
sisters. Only whereas Dimity revelled in the concept,
hero-worshipping him as she obviously did, Adair
found his attitude not only somewhat confusing,
but if she was truthful, utterly frustrating as well!
She didn't want to be treated as if she was his sister!
Although just how she *did* want him to behave
towards her—she had been the one to claim uninterest, after all—she wasn't certain she could have
spelt out with any assurance.

The nevertheless disquieting thought did occur
to her that, having once again proved that he was
more than capable of annihilating her defences,
Thane perhaps considered he had made his point
and therefore she didn't represent a challenge to
him any more.

Consequently, when next the whole household
prepared to travel in to town for polocrosse practice,
Adair resolutely donned a sloppy sweater of an unprepossessing putty colour, together with her baggy
fatigue pants and battle-jacket, and presented
herself on the veranda with a touch of defiance in
her stance as the last of the horses was being loaded
on to the specially rigged truck that was used to
transport them. Now let him think he had won! she
decided.

Seeing her, Thane slammed the bolt home on the tail-gate of the truck and strode in her direction with his mouth setting into a hard line. Adair even fancied a hostile glint entered his eyes, but because of the shade created by the brim of his bush hat she couldn't be certain, although she did experience a sudden shiver of apprehension just the same as he came to a halt on the other side of the veranda railing.

'What are you doing, wearing those?' His voice was quiet enough, but a muscle jerked spasmodically beside his tightened jaw.

Adair pressed her lips together—to stop them giving a betraying quiver?—and affected a nonchalant shrug. 'I felt like it,' she replied in challenging accents.

'For any particular reason?'

'It seemed a good idea at the time.'

Thane drew an audible breath and thrust his thumbs into the leather belt of his jeans. 'In order to prove...what?' He paused slightly longer, before adding sarcastically, *'This time!'*

Stung, Adair felt her own temper begin to rise. 'Nothing! I don't *need* to prove anything!' She swallowed hard. 'And nor do I require your permission regarding what I choose to wear!'

'Or any other—man's! Is that what you're trying to imply?'

If the rail and the insect screening hadn't separated them, Adair suspected he would have throttled her. 'And if it is?' she still dared to counter aggressively, regardless.

'Then I guess you've made your choice, and there's nothing more to say!' he bit out in cold,

inflexible tones that made her shiver, and swiv-
elling on his heel, he paced forcefully back to the
truck.

Adair watched him moodily, sighing as her brief
spurt of anger abruptly died. She might have succeeded in convincing him he had no victory to cel-
ebrate, but she surely didn't feel as if she had,
either! Moreover, neither had she expected quite
such an antagonistic reaction, and it was that more
than anything that served to overtake her feeling
of dismay with an increasingly mutinous resentment as the afternoon progressed. After all,
even if she had provoked the argument, that still
didn't give him any rights where she was concerned!

So it was that when, after their practice session
was concluded, Miles Pearson asked her to stay in
town and have dinner with him that evening, in an
impulsive rush of defiance, she agreed. Ever since
he had first met her at Ashvale's carnival, Miles
had made it quite evident he was interested in
furthering her acquaintance, but in spite of her
giving him no encouragement until now, she had
to admit that, as casual company, he seemed
pleasant enough. And if Thane Callahan had any
objections then he could console himself with
Rachel! she decided pungently, that girl once again
doing her utmost to monopolise every male within
distance in her customary syrupy manner.

However, when she told the others she wouldn't
be returning to the property until later in the
evening, and why, Thane made no comment whatsoever. He simply regarded her with the same stony
expression he had reserved for her all afternoon,
and she was reminded of once having accused him

of being both relentless and ruthless. Now, it
seemed she hadn't known just how much, until he
began employing those very same characteristics to
ignore her. And it hurt! she was forced to concede
reluctantly, even though she tried valiantly to dis-
regard it by occupying her attention elsewhere.

Nor did it make for a particularly enjoyable
evening either, she discovered, for as soon as there
was a lull in the conversation her thoughts inevitably returned to Thane. Not that Miles appeared
to notice her periods of preoccupation, and for that
she was grateful. She knew it would have been impossible to explain them away satisfactorily.
However, she wasn't sorry when the evening finally
came to an end and he drove her back the forty-
odd miles to Castlereagh. At least, not until her
stomach proceeded to twist itself into knots at the
sight of Thane leaning against a veranda post—
alerted by the sound of the approaching vehicle,
she supposed—when Miles brought them to a halt
a short distance from the steps.

'And just what was that for?' she demanded
tightly a few minutes later, after Thane had greeted
the younger man and summarily seen him on his
way again. 'He might at least have been invited in
for a cup of coffee, or something!'

'And perhaps give him the wrong idea?' Thane
countered as they mounted the steps, his tone
loaded with sarcasm. 'I was sure you wouldn't want
that.'

Adair drew a deep breath. 'Despite the fact that
it wasn't your decision to make!'

'Although it was in line with all your previous assertions!' His gaze raked over her derogatorily. 'Or is a wedding now in the offing?'

She came to a standstill before the front door, shaking her head. 'I don't know what you're talking about?'

'Try... your much cited theories concerning fidelity, etcetera!' he suggested in biting accents. 'After all, you seemed to think David's one-weekend association with Stephanie should have signified eternal faithfulness! So why not your evening with Miles too?'

'It's not the same!'

'Why? Because it's you doing it on this occasion? Because it's apparently only men's casual relationships that you despise so much?' He paused, his lips curling with contempt. 'You know what you are, don't you? Nothing but a mealy-mouthed bloody hypocrite!'

Adair's cheeks burned as much as her temper. 'Then I'm sure it will provide you with as much pleasure as it will me, if you just stay out of my life once and for all!'

Thane dipped his head sharply. 'You're so right!' he ground out with savage derision and, entering the wide hallway, strode down its length at a furious pace.

Shaken by the sheer violence contained in his voice, Adair found her throat tightening painfully, and she desperately tried to ignore the anguish that welled uncontrollably within her as she slowly began making her way to her room. Oh, God, what had she done? she lamented, closing the door behind her and collapsing on to her bed. She had finally succeeded in alienating him altogether...and promptly discovered, too late, that that wasn't what she wanted at all!

A sob rose in her throat. It was a shattering experience to suddenly have to admit that, far from disliking him, at that moment she wanted him desperately; that she needed him as she needed air to breathe; and that no matter how hard she had attempted to pretend otherwise, she was hopelessly in love with him!

Despite Adair's efforts the following morning to effect at least some sort of reconciliation with Thane—initially by wearing the most becoming casual outfit she had brought with her and having both her clothes and herself icily ignored—her emotions had eventually become somewhat ambivalent. On the one hand, despondency had enveloped her; but on the other, an angry resentment had surfaced too, at least part of which was directed towards herself.

It was all very well attempting to attract him now that she had finally realised, and admitted, she was in love with him, but she also had to admit that Thane had certainly never given any indication that he might love her in return either. Probably the opposite, in fact. Oh, he might have shown a desire to sleep with her, but that was hardly a declaration of undying devotion. One didn't necessarily have to be *in* love to *make* love!

Or had he actually warned her that was how it would be? she pondered heavily, suddenly remembering the time at the carnival when he had told her not to be so intense. Could he have been telling her then that he had no time for anything but casual, free and easy relationships, only she had been too involved with her own ideas to realise it? Just the fact that he had reached the age he had without marrying was surely an obvious indication that he was in no hurry to relinquish his independence!

Those last depressing thoughts had Adair stiffening her spine and coming to a decision. A heart-wrenching decision, but a decision, notwithstanding. If he wanted to play it cool, then so would she. When all was said and done, she did still have some pride and self-respect left!

So it was that when they were all seated in the living-room after dinner that evening and the coffee had been made, Adair made a point of being the one to hand Thane his. Together with the muted but dulcetly caustic comment, 'You don't have to say thanks. I do realise you would rather pretend I wasn't here!'

'Could I be that lucky?' he immediately retorted on a low, grating note, his eyes the shade of cold steel as they ranged over her disparagingly.

A thorn of pain lodged in Adair's chest, but she still managed to keep her chafing smile in place, if only with a supreme effort. 'Don't despair. You won't even have to pretend after tomorrow,' she mocked, and returned to her own seat to deliberately start up a laughing conversation with Dimity.

And that seemed to set the pattern for her last day on the property as well. Whenever they spoke it became a verbal duel—with an undercurrent of antagonistic, biting sarcasm—so that by the time Adair retired to her room to do her packing the following evening, the strain of striving to appear unaffected by it all was more than beginning to tell. She felt as if her every emotion was raw and lacerated!

When a knock came on her door some time later, she had still only listlessly packed a few items and, supposing it to be either Narelle or Dimity, she bade them enter in careless tones. When the door opened however, it was Thane's tall form and not her sister's or niece's that moved into the room, although only a short way.

Unprepared for his appearance, Adair stared at him with wide and defenceless eyes. 'Y-yes?' she stammered throatily.

He flexed a muscular shoulder impassively. 'Since I'll be gone before you leave in the morning, I thought I'd better at least say goodbye,' he relayed in sardonic tones.

'But—but I thought you were flying us back to Ashvale!' The surprised exclamation was forced from her.

'Yeah—well, now my father is instead.'

Her emotions churned, and she bent her head. He really couldn't wait to be rid of her. 'I see.' She swallowed with difficulty. 'So we won't be seeing each other again?'

An uneven tilt caught at his mouth. 'A comforting prospect, I'm sure you will agree!'

Actually, it made her feel empty, regretful, and just plain desolated! 'Thane...?' She took an impulsive step forward, her eyes searching his momentarily, before dropping again beneath the hard challenge she saw there. 'Do we—really have to part as—as...enemies?' she whispered achingly.

'*Part* as...!' A humourless laugh issued from deep in his darkly tanned throat. 'When have you ever considered me anything else?'

Adair dragged in a shaky breath. 'I admit I did most of the time, but...' she hesitated, 'not always, Thane! Not always!'

'No?' He arched a sardonic brow. 'Well, I guess I must have missed those few brief lapses!'

'Or you purposely ignored them!' she charged in retaliation for the pain his mocking dismissal of her confession had wrought.

'If that was the case... a good thing for both of us, it would appear!'

Adair's eyes began to mist betrayingly, and she turned away quickly with her arms wrapping about her midriff. She was obviously just wasting her time. 'Apparently,' she choked in muffled tones at last. And burst into tears as she heard the door slam.

# CHAPTER NINE

MAKING for the bed on unsteady legs, Adair caught a movement from the corner of her eye that had her spinning around with a gasp, and brushing her fingers frantically across her wet cheeks on seeing Thane pacing further into the room. 'I thought you'd gone,' she blurted bemusedly.

His shapely mouth took on an oblique cast. 'I suspect I'll regret that I didn't,' he owned on a heavily released breath.

She moved her head from side to side, her eyes shadowed pools of deep blue between their fringes of glossily wet lashes as she watched his approach. 'Then why are you—still here?'

Thane shrugged. 'Maybe I'm just a sucker for females in tears. Or maybe crying just doesn't seem in character for you.' He rubbed a hand around the back of his neck roughly and shook his head. 'Who the hell knows? I was only aware that I didn't want to leave you—like this,' he replied tautly, touching a still damp cheek with gentle fingers.

'And I—I didn't want you to l-leave either.' Her voice began to shake uncontrollably, and with a low groan he dragged her to him compulsively, his hands sliding into her hair on either side of her face as his mouth descended to take possession of hers with a scorching hunger.

Unable to resist, not wanting to, Adair melted pliantly against him, her arms reaching around his

177

broad back to hold him tightly, her lips parting and moving beneath his in open invitation. Clinging to him, she needed the comfort and security only his nearness could provide.

'Oh, God, why do I let you do this to me?' Thane muttered thickly against a corner of her mouth.

Her breath caught in her throat. 'You don't want to—kiss me?'

She could feel his whole body tense. 'God, yes!' he growled in roughened tones, and claimed her mouth again as if unable to help himself. 'But that isn't all I want! I also want *you* . . . in my arms, in my bed!' He shook his head impatiently. 'Hell, I also want some sanity back in my life, because I don't think I've had a rational thought since you walked into it!'

Her curling lashes fanned down to create hazy shadows across her creamy cheeks. 'So what do you intend to do about it?' she murmured unevenly.

'I know what I'd like to do!'

The depth of feeling in his voice had her eyes flicking upwards once more, and, emboldened by the smouldering desire in his expression, as well as her own heightened emotions, she reached up to nibble tantalisingly at his lower lip. 'Promise . . . ?' she whispered provocatively.

Thane's chest rose and fell heavily. 'I'm not in the mood for any more games, Adair!' he warned with a shuddering rasp.

'Nor am I,' she breathed shakily, and her eyes began to fill with tears once more. 'Oh, Thane . . . ! I didn't want to argue with you . . . it just seemed to happen! And—and I tried to make up for at least part of it early yesterday, but you just shut me out completely!'

Thane crushed her to him even more tightly, one hand stroking her bright hair soothingly. 'I didn't want to argue with you, or shut you out either, angel,' he confessed on the deepest of notes, his breath stirring the tendrils of hair at her temple. 'But I had to do something to try and stop you tearing me apart altogether! I just couldn't take it any more!'

Adair burrowed her head closer against his chest. 'And—now?' she ventured to enquire tentatively.

Drawing her head back a space, he began kissing the wetness from her lashes with an unhurried, arousing sensuousness. 'Now...?' He turned his attention to her trembling lips to trace their contours with the tip of his tongue, and every breath she took was filled with the warm taste and pleasing smell of him. 'Now it kills me to even think what life without you might be like!'

'Oh, Thane!' Her hands slid up to twine about his neck lovingly, and it was she who kissed him now—with an instinctive sexuality she hadn't even known she possessed. She loved him, and she wanted him more than she would ever have believed it possible to want any man. And her mounting desire wasn't lost on him.

In one swift movement Thane gathered her up into his arms, then he was depositing her on the bed. Adair's heart pounded as his mouth reclaimed hers, this time with an increasing demand and urgency that turned her blood to fire, and she responded willingly. Suddenly she remembered from before the exciting feel of his bare skin against hers, and she yearned to experience the same again. To touch him, and to feel his hard and sinewed form pressed so close to hers.

As if sensing her longings, or perhaps because they aligned with his own, Thane began removing her clothing gently, all the while covering each newly exposed area of silken skin with warm, tormenting kisses, so that she was feverish with wanting by the time he had finished, and had disposed of his own garments. Then his mouth was covering hers again with a deepening intensity, and she clasped him to her eagerly. He had a marvellously strong body, muscular, bronzed, and powerfully male, and she couldn't resist running her hands over the smooth, firm flesh.

With a groan, Thane slid his hands down her back, taking pleasure from the feel of her flawless skin, then, smoothing across her slender, rounded hips, they moved leisurely upwards once more to cup and caress her swelling breasts. Adair arched against him helplessly, feeling as if she was melting beneath his hands, and her fingers dug deep into his dark hair when his mouth and tongue found her already throbbing nipples, torturing them with sensation until she couldn't control the soft moan of ecstatic pleasure that escaped her.

She ached for the release she knew only his total possession could bring, but when he moved his long length over her she sucked in a ragged breath and buried her face against the side of his throat. 'Be gentle,' she breathed shyly. 'I—I've never done—this before.'

Tensing, Thane eased her head away from his neck with one hand, his darkened grey eyes searching hers wonderingly, his fingers caressng the delicate line of her jaw. 'You're a virgin?'

Adair swallowed and nodded.

His brows drew together slightly. 'But with you having been engaged, I just assumed...' He paused. 'Then why me...now?'

She trailed her fingers across his hard chest, a transient half-smile lighting her face, although her gaze didn't quite meet his. 'I guess you must mean more to me than he ever did,' she owned, and now she did look up at him, expressively, from between her long curling lashes.

Thane's softening expression had a current of joy rippling through her. 'Oh, Adair, I love you!' he vowed in a voice heavy with pent-up passion, but when his lips came down on hers it was with a tender, carefully controlled hunger, and Adair knew she had been right in waiting for just such a man before committing herself so completely.

Now, slowly, gently, Thane used his mouth and his hands to bring her body to the peak of desire, stimulating every nerve and fibre of her being until she thought she would die from sheer wanting, and only then skilfully fusing his body with hers. The pain of his penetration had her instinctively trying to draw back, and he paused, his hands gentling her, his mouth persuasively reassuring as it moved on hers. Then he began moving again, moving deeper inside her, languidly almost at first, giving her time to become accustomed to the feel of him, and then gradually the rhythm quickened as she intuitively tightened about him—again and again— in a fervent response to his sexual knowledge.

Adair felt his body shudder against hers at the same time as she began to shake with the intensity of feeling overwhelming her. An explosion of feeling that made the world spin as they crested together, blending as one, and soaring to heights of rapture the like of which she could never have imagined.

Afterwards, they lay curled together as their breathing gradually slowed, and Adair supposed they must have slept, or at least she had, for the next time she became aware of her surroundings the temperature of the room was much cooler.

Stirring drowsily, she nestled closer to the warmth of Thane's hard body beneath the covers she deduced he must have pulled over them, her eyes flickering open languorously. Her cheek was resting against a solidly muscled shoulder, one arm flung across his broad chest, and seemingly of their own accord her fingers began to trail experimentally over the hard muscles.

'Hmm... I must say, I like the manner in which you wake up,' she suddenly heard Thane declare with husky humour, and her eyes lifted to his in surprise to find him regarding her lazily in the dim glow of the bedside lamp that was still alight.

'I didn't realise you were awake,' she half smiled shyly, flushing.

The upward curve of his lips became more pronounced. 'If I hadn't been initially, I'm sure I very soon would have been,' he drawled meaningfully, making her colour heighten. 'Although the matter that possibly interests me most at the moment is...' his gaze sobered somewhat and turned watchful,

'... whether you're prepared to take another chance on reaching the altar.'

She drew a deep breath. 'With you?'

His mouth shaped ruefully. 'I'm certainly not here on anyone's else behalf.' Easing her upwards so that she was half lying across him, he threaded his fingers within her hair and then urged her head lower, his lips feathering lightly, tantalisingly, over her own. 'So what's the answer to be, angel?'

Despite the fact that her heart was pounding, Adair still hesitated briefly, unable to entirely overcome the memories that suddenly assailed her. 'You're positive that's what you—really want?'

Thane's eyes softened tenderly with understanding at her tentativeness, but his reply was as reassuring as she could have wished. 'Oh, hell, yes!'

There were no restrictions on the rapture that now bubbled inside her, and it showed in the glow of her adoring eyes. 'Oh, Thane, I love you so!' she breathed devoutly.

'Meaning... you will marry me?'

'Yes, oh yes!' Her voice shook a little with happiness. 'Today, in fact, if it were possible!'

'I only wish to God it were!' he concurred deeply, bringing her mouth down to his once more, and it was a long time before either of them experienced the wish to do anything except express their feelings in the most satisfying way possible.

'You know...' It was Adair who first began to speak, in a partly musing, partly amused tone, some considerable time later. 'This definitely wasn't the outcome I envisioned on first meeting you... you interfering bastard!' Her accompanying smile made the word more of an endearment than a disparagement. 'Always refusing to allow me to dress or act as I wanted, and then making me want to please *you*! Invading my life to such an extent that when I didn't see you at all for a couple of days after— after that night at the motel, I hardly knew what to think any more. I just knew I missed you, and...' she took a deep breath before confessing, 'hated Rachel for being with you!'

The arms about her tightened. 'You had no need to,' Thane assured her huskily. 'Rachel invited herself along with us. I've never invited her *any-where* with me!' He exhaled deeply. 'And you couldn't possibly have missed me more than I did you, believe me! Nor were you the only one needing to do some thinking after that night either.' He shook his head. 'Lord, I knew that you'd piqued my interest—that I thought it a tragic waste for someone with your looks to deliberately try to disguise them—but I sure wasn't prepared for the effect you had on me that night either, love.' Supporting his head on his hand, he looked down at her mock-censuringly. 'Nor, might I add, did our first evening here do anything to help solve the problem!'

'So thereafter you treated me like a kid sister instead!' Adair wrinkled her nose in wry disgust. 'A most frustrating experience I wouldn't like to have to repeat, I can tell you!'

'Don't worry, I can't imagine you ever having to,' Thane returned with an evocative grin. 'But at the time I was finding it extremely difficult to know just *how* to treat you. You would appear to be giving way, but then you would immediately retreat once more. I couldn't force myself on you...no matter how much the idea appealed on occasion,' he inserted, ruefully honest, 'so I thought the only way left to me was to wait for you to give *me* a signal of some kind. Then it seemed you did...' He raised an expressive shoulder.

'My clothes—the day of your polocrosse practice,' she deduced on a regretful sigh. 'The only trouble was, I merely did that in order to try to gain a different reaction from you!' Her mouth took on a wry shape. 'Though not the kind it did receive!'

He tilted her head slightly, his mouth finding hers and lingering. 'I'm sorry, but I'm afraid I wasn't feeling too kindly disposed towards you at the time,' he admitted heavily. 'I was coming to hate the hold you seemed to have over me, the way you could turn me inside out at will.'

'Oh, Thane, if only I'd known!' Adair shook her head sorrowfully. 'But I thought you simply saw me as a challenge to—to your ego because of my supposed attitude towards men.'

He eyed her narrowly. 'I'll let that first part pass for the time being, but...supposed?' His brows rose sceptically.

She half smiled self-consciously. 'Well, maybe not altogether. Although I think I've known for some time, subsconsciously at least, that you were different. That you meant something special to me.' She swallowed, averting her gaze. 'Unfortunately, it wasn't until we had that last argument, and I thought I'd alienated you for ever, that I finally admitted just how special.'

Thane caught her to him comfortingly. 'That being the night you had dinner with Miles Pearson, as I recall.'

'Yes—well...' She eyed him contritely, but on seeing the lazily wry look on his face, dimpled, and dared to quiz, 'Were you jealous?'

'Very!' he owned succinctly.

'You shouldn't have been so cold towards me, then, should you?'

'Witch!' he charged with a heart-shaking smile, and took his revenge in a fashion they both welcomed. On releasing her, he smiled crookedly. 'But if you're not careful, you'll have me here all night!' And he began pushing himself into a sitting position.

Adair frowned, her expression becoming tinged with doubt. 'You don't want to stay?'

'Do I!' he retorted gruffly, pressing her back against the pillows and capturing her lips so hungrily that she was breathless, and in no doubt whatsoever, by the time he relinquished them. Then he brushed the back of his fingers across her cheek, a whimsical smile tugging at the corners of his mouth. 'But since it's more than a probability that the old man will come looking for me early in the morning, I think you at least would find it less embarrassing if he discovered me in my own room rather than yours. Besides which, and even though I'm afraid there's no guarantee after this, I somehow suspect you would still prefer not to be a very pregnant bride, if at all possible.'

Adair coloured. Until then she hadn't really given the possibility a thought. And if the latter did happen to be the case, it really would be the end as far as her mother was concerned, she knew. But more importantly... 'Would you—mind?' she questioned hesitantly.

Thane framed her face between his hands and kissed her unhurriedly. 'Only in so far as I'd rather have you to myself for a while,' he said softly.

Reassured, she expelled the breath she hadn't realised she had been holding, and laughed. '*Will* that be possible, anyway, when Narelle marries your father?'

'You'd better believe it!' he grinned as he slid from under the covers and she watched possessively, admiring the unconscious strength and grace exhibited in every movement of his powerful form as he dressed. 'There's no lack of space here, fortunately. We can take a whole wing for our own suite of rooms.'

A sudden thought occurred and she couldn't help but giggle. 'Do you realise, my father-in-law will also be my brother-in-law?'

He nodded. 'And my sister-in-law will also be my stepmother.' Which thought had them both laughing. Then, finished dressing, he turned to rest one knee on the edge of the bed and leant over her, a hand on either side of her head. 'But now...' He eyed her ruefully.

Adair sighed and clasped her hands around his neck. 'You couldn't stay for just a little longer?'

'A *little* longer?' Thane stressed in something of a growl. 'Hell! How strong do you think my resolve is?'

Adair moved her head from side to side. 'But when will I see you again?' she wailed.

'In the morning, of course,' he smiled, and bent to kiss her lightly. 'You didn't really think I wouldn't be flying you home after this, did you?' His smile widened disarmingly. 'Besides, I have something to discuss with your parents—or, more particularly, your father—and *we* have arrangements to make for a wedding...in the very near future too, I hope, because I can see myself rapidly reaching the stage where I don't give a damn if we tempt fate once too often or not!' he concluded with a groan, and this time when his mouth found hers it was with a smouldering desire.

'You don't regret not having left, after all, then?' Adair murmured piquantly at length. And after his half smiling, half frowning look in response, she elucidated with an openly teasing smile, 'Earlier, you said you suspected you'd regret it.'

Now his smile subdued his frown altogether, but not the inherent huskiness in his voice as he averred tenderly, 'Although not as much as I regret having to leave now, believe me!' He caught hold of one of her hands and pressed his lips sensuously to its palm. 'But I'd better—while I still can! So go to sleep, angel, and I'll see you in the morning.' Releasing her hand, he gained his feet once more.

Although she sighed at the thought of his imminent departure, the upward curve catching at her mouth was still a contented one. 'I'll dream about you,' she promised softly.

Thane put a forefinger to his lips and touched it gently to hers. 'With you on my mind, I doubt *I'll* sleep at all!' he retorted in throaty tones, and, turning on his heel, made for the door swiftly. Before he changed his mind, seemingly!

When the door had closed behind him, Adair switched off the lamp and snuggled further down beneath the covers. Her last thought before sleep claimed her was a recollection of Thane having once

# Harlequin Romance

## Coming Next Month

**2935  TRUST IN LOVE  Jeanne Allan**
Fleeing from malicious, career-threatening rumors, successful model Kate returns to her small Nebraska hometown. There, unexpected help from onetime town rebel Ty Walker makes her stop running and fight back.

**2936  PLAYING SAFE  Claudia Jameson**
Demetrius Knight disapproves of Grace Allinson—which suits her perfectly. After one heartbreak she has no desire to get involved again. Unfortunately his young sister's needs make it hard for Grace to befriend her while determinedly ignoring her brother!

**2937  FEELINGS  Margaret Mayo**
Melissa, for good reasons, isn't interested in any man—much less someone like Benedict Burton, who demands that she scrap her adopted Miss Mouse appearance to be like the pretty, vivacious women he prefers!

**2938  ONE-WOMAN MAN  Sue Peters**
Radio Deejay Berry Baker can't understand why her fund-raising plan for a children's ward at St. Luke's Hospital has turned into a contest for control—between herself and Julian Vyse, the senior medical consultant. But the battle lines are clearly drawn....

**2939  MORNING GLORY  Margaret Way**
Someday young, talented Kit Lacey knows a man will come along to match her zest for life. And when Thorne Stratton, international news correspondent, arrives in Queensland's Eden Cove, he exactly fits the bill. Convincing him, Kit finds, is quite another matter.

**2940  NEPTUNE'S DAUGHTER  Anne Weale**
Oliver Thornton is a name out of Laurian's past, and one she has every reason to hate. When Oliver turns up once more in her life, she's wary. Surely he will only break her heart—again!

Available in October wherever paperback books are sold, or through Harlequin Reader Service:

In the U.S.
901 Fuhrmann Blvd.
P.O. Box 1397
Buffalo, N.Y.  14240-1397

In Canada
P.O. Box 603
Fort Erie, Ontario
L2A 5X3

suggested that her ex-fiancé might have done her a favour by jilting her. At the time she had been scornful of the suggestion, but now... Now she couldn't possibly have agreed more, and she smiled blissfully...

## Ron Jaworski

| Team | Year | | | | | | | |
|---|---|---|---|---|---|---|---|---|
| Los Angeles | 1973 | TAXI SQUAD | | | | | | |
| Los Angeles | 1974 | 24 | 10 | 41.7 | 144 | 0 | 1 | 6.0 |
| Los Angeles | 1975 | 48 | 24 | 50.0 | 302 | 0 | 2 | 6.3 |
| Los Angeles | 1976 | 52 | 20 | 28.5 | 273 | 1 | 5 | 5.2 |
| Philadelphia | 1977 | 346 | 166 | 48.0 | 2,183 | 18 | 21 | 6.3 |
| Philadelphia | 1978 | 398 | 206 | 51.8 | 2,487 | 16 | 16 | 6.2 |
| Philadelphia | 1979 | 374 | 190 | 50.8 | 2,669 | 18 | 12 | 7.1 |
| Philadelphia | 1980 | 451 | 257 | 57.0 | 3,529 | 27 | 12 | 7.8 |
| Pro Totals | | 1,693 | 873 | 51.6 | 11,587 | 80 | 69 | 6.8 |

## Steve Bartkowski

| Team | Year | | | | | | | |
|---|---|---|---|---|---|---|---|---|
| Atlanta | 1975 | 255 | 115 | 45.1 | 1,662 | 13 | 15 | 6.5 |
| Atlanta | 1976 | 120 | 57 | 47.5 | 677 | 2 | 9 | 5.5 |
| Atlanta | 1977 | 136 | 64 | 47.1 | 796 | 5 | 13 | 5.8 |
| Atlanta | 1978 | 369 | 187 | 50.7 | 2,489 | 10 | 18 | 6.7 |
| Atlanta | 1979 | 379 | 203 | 53.6 | 2,502 | 17 | 20 | 6.6 |
| Atlanta | 1980 | 463 | 257 | 55.5 | 3,544 | 31 | 16 | 7.6 |
| Pro Totals | | 1,722 | 883 | 51.3 | 11,670 | 78 | 91 | 6.8 |